LOSING LIAM

J. A. WYNTERS

Editing by: Spell bound editing

Cover design: The Dust Jacket Designs

Interior Formatting: Dawn Lucous, Yours Truly Book Services

One day.

Whether you are 14, 28 or 65 you will stumble upon someone who will start a fire in you that cannot die.

However, the saddest, most awful truth you will ever come to find is they are not always with whom we spend our lives. –Beau Taplin

EVIE

Missing you doesn't come in waves. It's a battering ram into my chest that smashes my insides every time your name passes like a ghost inside my mind. It makes it hard to breathe, to take another step forward. It makes everything hurt, and sitting with that pain makes me want to rip out my heart and catapult it away. Instead, it drips slowly inside me, poisoning me with sadness. Sadness I have no right to feel. But I can't help how empty I am without you.

This is a story about a boy, but I guess you already know that. The one who got away, the one who was never really mine to begin with. If only I'd known then that love is so short and forgetting is endless, I might have protected myself better, built higher walls, pushed away these feelings that crept like a thief in the night, unseen and unheard until it was too late; until they were so deep-seated inside me I could not escape them. But as always, I am starting in the middle. So let me take you back to the beginning.

About a boy.

Maybe I was lucky. Meeting the love of my life by chance so young had to be luck. With almost seven and a half billion people on the planet, finding *the one* had to be more than just a coincidence, a twist of fate, an accident, and yet somehow the universe propelled us together. Of course, when I first met him, I had no idea that he would hold my heart forever. He was only a boy, and I was a girl, and our lives collided in a beautiful mess.

Summers were always my favourite. In the way the sun caressed my face and the light breeze brushed away the edges of the heat. In the way the air was always full of the smell of burning sausages and sunscreen. In the shrieks and giggles kids made as they ran into the freezing water and the blaring of music from afternoon parties. There was something about summer that always sang to me like a favourite song you turn up really loud every time it comes on the radio, and you can't help but belt out the lyrics out of tune.

But the best thing about summer was Liam Morrison. I didn't know he would become so important to me. Not at first of course, not till that last summer. Not till the last

heartbreak, but then again, the best things creep up on us unexpectedly.

Blue Haven is a small beach town where the locals are fiercely protective of each other's secrets and not very welcoming to outsiders. There are no deep-seated dark pasts or a village tragedy that marred the area; they just like their peace on their spectacular piece of land. They shun the city folk and restrain the deluge of tourists who try to flood their town each summer. Twenty kilometres down the road you will find Angel Falls; its population exploded over the past fourteen years, and developers have sunk their teeth and bulldozers into the land, turning the idyllic seascape into a tourist haven that bursts beyond capacity every summer.

In contrast, the residents of Blue Haven chased away any would be developer, battled any offers for large hotels or new apartment buildings, and the deserted motel just two kilometres from the city limits is shrouded with questions as to why it was abandoned. The council members have kept their lips sealed about it, and all the locals have learnt not to ask. The ghostly half-built skeleton has become a place for tourists to wander about and for the local teenagers to hang out on weekends.

And that's where we are today, Liam and me. Looking up at the stars as if the rest of the world doesn't exist. And usually, when I'm here in his arms like this, I like to think that it doesn't. I like to think that we are the last and the only people around and that what we have, what we share is bigger than everyone else.

I've been coming to Blue Haven for the past ten years— since I was six years old. My grandfather owns a house across the road from the beach. Waking up to the lapping of gentle waves and the smell of salty humid air became as

familiar to me as the smell of my mother's rare hugs or my father's shoe polish every time he came home.

I met Liam just after my tenth birthday. He is a local, born and bred, and though at first, we were nothing more than friends, over time it evolved into so much more. Perhaps it was the way that he was just like summer; hot and sweet and fun. Perhaps it was the way he saw me in a way that no one else did. It really didn't matter. All that mattered was that whenever I was in Blue Haven, I knew I'd be in his arms, and it would feel like home.

"Next year I graduate," he whispers into my hairline as I snuggle closer into his chest.

"And...?"

"And? And then I'm free." I feel his lips tip up in a smile. I bet if I looked it would be bittersweet. Just like knowing this is the last day of my vacation. Tomorrow we'll pack up the car and wave goodbye to the rippling tides and lapping waves and head back to the city. To the hustle and bustle, the screeching of tyres at midnight and the incessant chatter of people on their phones.

"Free to do what?" I tease him, but my smile evaporates when he rolls above me. His dark hazel eyes are buried in shadows and his brow is creased in deep furrows.

"Free to come to you, to be near you every day. To kiss you." He smiles, and my heart ripples as he kisses me, gently and urgently all at once.

When his lips leave mine, I instantly miss them, just like I miss him any time he isn't within reach. "I can't wait to have you around every day."

"Yeah?" His face beams with a cocky smile.

"Yeah," I respond with one of my own as heat rushes through my body.

"And what would you do if you had me every day?" He

kisses that place where my neck meets my shoulders, and my skin erupts in goosebumps.

"Not sure I could put it into words." The heat in my face intensifies as I think of all the things I could do with Liam if I never had to let him go.

"Why don't you show me instead?" The question muffled against my hair, his hot breath on my skin leaves me burning.

He's been patient with me, slow. And though we've had plenty of opportunities, he's always held back, wanting me to be ready, to be sure. And tonight I am. If I have to wait another year before I have him all to myself again, I want us both to remember what the other felt like, tasted like, looked like.

I nod, and his eyes find mine, tender and creased with anxious nervousness that I am sure matches my own.

"Are you sure?" Muscles jump along his jaw.

I nod again, the nerves sealing the words in my throat.

He kisses me then. It's soft and slow and tender, and his lips on mine divulge just how much he loves me, wants me, needs me.

His shirt comes off next, and I take in his wide shoulders and athletic build. He's not a jock but lean, and his tanned body is tensed and bunched as he settles himself above me.

We're both inexperienced. I should be more afraid as adrenaline courses through my body and my nerves stand on edge, but what we share is something beautiful and intense. Looking up at Liam this close burns. I absorb every detail in a blink. His eyes hooded by shadows, his hair falling across his forehead that he holds to mine as the world holds its breath. For a short while, I leave my body and become a part of him, and all I know is that I wish I could put all my feelings in a bottle and capture them forever.

"I love you," he whispers, and his raw voice spikes a shiver that races through me.

"I love you too." And I do.

As always, Liam drops me off a few streets from my grandfather's house and I'm not walking, I'm flying. Gliding over the dark streets, a smile tugging at my lips. My heart flutters each time I think of Liam, of his lips and his smell and the way he makes me feel.

In the morning I'll pack up and we will have our traditional pancake breakfast before I get to sneak out and kiss him a final goodbye. A perfect end to a perfect summer.

It's well after midnight, and as I approach the house, I expect all the lights to be off and everyone to be asleep. Instead, there are flashing lights and a flurry of people running in and out, trying to remain calm. My mum stands at the threshold, tears streaming down her cheeks, and I run towards the house, panic eating at my chest.

"What happened?" I'm breathless as I reach the door, a second before paramedics walk out of the house pushing the gurney. My father is listless. Tubes and bags hanging off the bed as they rush him towards the ambulance.

"Where the hell were you?" is all she says as one of the paramedics tells her which hospital they are taking my father to. "Get in the car," she hisses at me, her venom stinging my skin.

I rush to the car and slam the door behind me. My mother is seconds behind, and she revs the engine before pulling out of the driveway like a madwoman.

"Where are we going? Can't I stay with grandad?"

She shoots me a hard look before her gaze snaps back to

the road. "No. They are taking your dad to the oval where the helicopter will fly him out to St. Vincent's."

My blood runs cold, and I don't know if it's because it's dawning on me that my dad is being rushed to a big city hospital because the smaller one in Angel Falls doesn't have the facilities to look after him, or because I'm realizing that tomorrow's goodbye is dissolving.

"What about my stuff?"

"You have more things at home."

"But—"

"You're so bloody selfish." Her tone cuts through me as fresh tears fall and run down her cheeks.

I bite my lower lip which suddenly quivers, and my heart stammers in my chest, tearing. Guilt gnaws at my core. Of course I worry for my father, still in the dark as to what's actually happened, but with every metre we drive, I'm farther away from Liam. I want to scream for him. I want him to be here with me, to hold me and tell me everything will be okay. I want him to kiss my forehead in the way that he does that lets me know the sun will rise again tomorrow, but we drive away and into darkness.

<hr>

I've sent him six messages and still, there is no reply. Everything hurts my heart, my body. I just need him as I pace the sterilised hospital corridor. It's amazing how a space so bare can feel so intimidating. By the time they got my dad to the ICU and injected him with tPA, it was too late. The clot had already done its damage and the stroke was far too severe. The man I once knew is gone. Seeing someone so viciously strong and capable crumble and deteriorate in a blink of an eye is a good way to extract your heart from your chest without lifting a finger.

The once solid military man that I grew up with vanished in a flash of red and blue lights, leaving behind an invalid. A man bedridden and incompetent who couldn't lift his hand, let alone go to the toilet. I knew when I saw him like that that he wouldn't last. His pride alone would strangle him. A man so used to think of himself like a king. A powerful force who others naturally followed and respected now reduced to a mere shadow dressed in adult diapers.

They should have let him die. It would have been a mercy.

My mother's angry silence is broken by the soft padded footsteps of the nurses moving from room to room and the occasional blaring alarm. Nothing moves fast here; this wing is for the hopeless and the broken. They brought us up here from the ICU a few hours ago, and the doctors had a long, whispered conversation with my mother. Her narrow, angry eyes kept darting to my face, piercing me with guilt.

Tears slide down my face as my insides churn, clammy fingers grip my heart, squeezing tight, threatening to push all the air out of my lungs till I struggle to breathe. I feel utterly alone. But before I can choke on my misery, warm familiar arms drape around me, and the smell of the ocean wraps itself around me. "I came as soon as I could." His muffled voice filters through my hair.

I spin to find Liam's concerned eyes and tired face. I have no idea how he is here, but I don't care as I throw myself at him and sob, soaking his shirt as I do. He doesn't release me, doesn't scold me; he just holds me and comforts me as I imagine a future without the father I once knew.

"What are you doing here?" My mother's cold voice slices between us, and I push myself away from Liam, noting the wet patch on his peck. His arm remains firmly on my waist.

"Good morning, Mrs Miller." He's formal and charming but remains forlorn.

"I asked what you're doing here." She ignores my wet face and silent sobs.

"Evie told me what happened. I thought she could use a friend."

She scoffs, and her eyes swing from him to me then back again, lingering for a few seconds on the arm that gives me strength.

"If she wasn't with her *friends* last night, she would have been home."

I feel his back bunch up and the muscles tense, but he remains passive and neutral. "I don't mean to step on any toes. I just wanted to offer my support."

"I'm sure you've offered my *underaged* daughter more than that," she hisses out at him, and my mouth falls open.

He ignores her scathing remark, and I envy him. I wish I could learn to be so impassive around her. His grip tightens on my waist staying just shy of painful. "When she comes of age, I would like to offer her everything."

My heart stumbles at his words, and I search his face, but he's looking at my mother whose mouth twists in disdain.

"She can do better."

"Mum!" I finally snap out of my subdued state and glare at her as darts of anger and disbelief hit my chest.

Liam turns to me; worry and anger crease his eyes. "It's okay, Evie." I shake my head, disagreeing. "I better go."

"But you just got here." I grab onto him, desperate, no longer concerned with my mother's scowl or harsh words.

"You should be with your family."

"You are my family."

His lips twitch in what could have been a smile and his hand squeezes my waist for a split second, but enough for me to feel that he feels the same way even if he can't voice it. For the first time since I've gotten to this place, I feel something resembling content.

"I better go."

"I'll walk you out," I offer and don't wait for my mother's rebuke before we head down the corridor, his hand slipping easily into mine as we walk in silence.

"I'm sorry—"

"No. It's okay. You've told me what she's like." I nod as he gathers me into his arms and holds me. I leach as much warmth and strength from him as I can and indulge in his scent. Sweat and salt and a hint of sunscreen hidden behind too much aftershave.

He releases me, and I'm loath to tear myself away from him. There is an instant lingering ache like I'm missing a part of myself. "You just got here; it would have taken you hours."

"It's okay, I borrowed my dad's car."

"Does he know?" A small smile creeps along his face and worry instantly eats at my chest. "He's going to kill you."

"It's worth it if I can be here with you." I bite down the emotion that claws its way up my throat. "You better get back inside."

I nod, not wanting to let him go but knowing the longer I remain out here with him, the more miserable my mother will make me.

He kisses the top of my head then my salty cheeks before he gifts me with a soft parting kiss. "I love you, Evie. I'll see you soon."

"I love you too," I croak, the floodgates of my grief and anger about to breach my barriers.

I watch him walk away and disappear amongst the cars in the lot. I want to scream his name. I want to run to him and melt into his chest where I know I can find comfort, but I don't. I let my shoulders sag, and I swallow down all my pain before I make my way back inside.

TWO YEARS LATER

EVIE

The phone pings, and I reach over to the nightstand to grab it. I read the text, huff out a frustrated sound and put the phone back down, snuggling back into Liam.

"Your mum?"

"Mm hm," I hum into his chest, not really wanting to talk about her while I curl up against his warm, naked body.

"What does she want?"

"The same thing as always; someone to blame." My hand reaches across his torso, and I cling to him. "Can we please not talk about her?" My lips brush over his chest.

He flips us over in a quick movement and settles between my legs. My favourite place for him to be as of late. "What would you rather be talking about then?" His lips capture mine in a soft kiss that erases all traces of her. And then it's just us again. Me and Liam and the power in his body, the persuasion in it. It's intoxicating.

"I have to get to class," I moan, not really wanting to leave our bed, not wanting to leave him.

"Okay." He pretends like he didn't hear me at all.

His warm fingers brush my jaw, and I melt against his touch. My own hands sink into his hair before they travel the length of his strong back. He leans in, our foreheads touching, and the heat of his breath feathers my lips before he gives me one of his cocky smiles. They are my favourite; they scream mischief and fun with a little arrogance for good measure.

His velvety lips find my skin. They are soft and warm as they kiss a path along my jaw dipping down to my neck and along my collarbone. My nails dig into his back, and he releases a raspy breath before working his way back up, his tongue slipping out of his mouth and tasting my skin, teasing it. My skin tingles as he works his way up to my mouth sealing it with his, devouring me in a hungry kiss as his hard length pushes against me, again and again.

God, I love the way he kisses me, like every part of me belongs to him. The way he invades my mouth, with the possessive flicks of his tongue guiding my movement and swallowing my moans. Powering through me, demanding that I feel his kiss in every part of my body, in the tips of my fingers that latch onto his back, or the arch of my neck that wants more of his mouth or in the aching throb between my legs.

His hands touch my body, freely. He knows that I belong to him, wholly. He brings his weight down on me and kisses my cheek again, his hot breath fanning my skin. His hips spread my legs wider and his breath burns my skin. He rocks against me, grinding, thrusting, till he finds entry and he's inside me with one hard powerful push.

My spine bows, and he growls against my skin, "Fuck." He nips at my flesh before pulling out slowly and plunging again, over and over. My teeth find his shoulder and my nails claw at his back, leaving long furrows down his back as his thrusts push me closer to the edge of pleasure.

My thighs clamp around his hips, matching his speed and movements, and all I know is that I need him faster, deeper, harder. His pace becomes erratic and fitful till he buries himself to the root, clutching at my shoulders, his chopped breath against my neck as his body sags.

He rests his forehead against my shoulder and his breath settles. He peeks at me from beyond his hair. "I'm sorry, I wanted you to…"

I kiss away his apology. "I know."

"Evie." His velvet lips capture mine in a long intoxicating kiss, and my throbbing pussy aches with need.

I push him away, not because I have any desire to detach myself from him but because I have to get to class. "I have to go."

Liam doesn't release me, instead, he presses down on me, and his fingers dig into my flesh as he lowers himself down, then buries his face between my thighs. His tongue lashes out, and my sensitive clit comes to life at the slight flicker. I moan, bucking my hips against his mouth while his tongue punishes me and his fingers bury themselves deep inside me. He licks and kisses, and his fingers move inside me till I crumble under the pleasure. I come hard and fast. Wave after wave of pleasure washes over me, my hands bunching the sheet between tightened fists, and his name toppling from my lips like a desperate prayer.

Slowly I find air in the room, and when I open my eyes, Liam is on his knees between my legs. Sweat sheets his torso, and his mouth glistens around a satisfied smile. "Now you can go." He winks at me, and I groan, melting into the mattress.

I don't want to leave.

L iving with Liam is like a fairy tale. It's the stuff dreams are made of and everyone covets. It's in the little things really; the way he kisses my shoulder as he grabs something off the dinner plate I'm not yet finished cooking. It's the way he makes me a coffee at ten at night knowing I have to stay up for a few more hours to study. It's the way that even when he comes home exhausted after his shift, he makes time for me, even if that means falling asleep on the couch while I snuggle into his warm body. And it's in all the ways he fucks me. In the shower, on the kitchen bench, in our bed, over the railing of the stairwell that one time when he couldn't wait to get in the door. It's all the small ways that he shows me he loves me. And I love him too, dearly. He is my family, my future, my fucking everything.

When he moved up to the city a two years ago and found me, I thought my heart would never stop thundering. I was elated, and my mother was annoyed. And when I turned eighteen and he was twenty, there was nothing she could do to stop us moving in together.

Our flat was small and cramped and everything we ever wanted. It was a stepping stone to a future we would build together. It was the two-room matchbox place we would one day look back on and remember with fondness. It was our origin story.

Liam worked in a factory. I knew he hated it. I knew he missed the outdoors and the waves he surfed on every day since he was kid. I knew he missed the sun kissing his skin and the salt water cooling it. But he kept saying he didn't care, and that after I finished school, we could look at moving closer to the beach again. I believed him, even though every now and then I caught him staring at the blue skies with melancholy notes in his eyes.

I wonder if I knew then what I know now if I would do

anything different. If I would say more or less. If I'd commit so much more to memory, or if I'd take the time to dwell on each detail and let it be etched into my memory like a tattoo instead of a shadow, one that's always with me but changes as time moves on. I often go back to that time and try to grab on to that feeling, that unadulterated joy, uncorrupted by time or age or baggage. It was so perfect, and no other feeling has ever matched it, none has ever come close. I wonder how I would have done things differently—or maybe I wouldn't have—maybe they were perfect just as they were.

But that morning when he left for work—I often ask myself if I would have kissed him harder? Longer? If I should have told him I loved him one more time. Would any of it matter now?

The thing about last times is that you never know they are the last. You take them for granted, assuming things will evolve with time but never really change. You assume the people you love will always be there because they love you back, because you are their home, their heart. And when bad things happen, they happen to other people because you've already had your share of tragedy.

Liam disappeared on a Thursday. It was just another day. We shared a moment in bed where he just held me like I was his whole world and he kissed me goodbye as he did every day, parting with one of his quirky smiles that assured me everything will be okay.

That day is etched in my mind like a heart in a tree trunk, carved deep and meticulously. My classes dragged on, and my sandwich collapsed onto the floor, the lettuce soaking through the bread rendering it a soggy useless mess.

I made dinner; fish and oven-baked chips with veg on the side. I didn't really need the vegetables, but Liam always insisted, and then I waited, watching the food turn a shade of grey as it grew cold. He was two hours late. But I wasn't worried, not yet. He'd been late before. But he didn't call, and when I did, the phone went straight to voicemail. I put it down to a dead battery and watched the news, then some comedy show.

After four hours, a worm of panic crawled inside me and settled in the pit of my stomach. I found myself looking at the door more and more, jumping at any sound and running to the window.

After the sixth hour, the worm had managed to gnaw its way across my abdomen and had multiplied. My stomach twisted and knotted with the feeling of them wriggling inside me, and all I felt was a sick sense of trepidation.

I called his boss and apologised for the late hour. When he told me Liam left work early and in a rush, my stomach plummeted.

I call his sister, but just like Liam's, her phone goes straight to voicemail. I leave a frantic message and try him for the hundredth time.

"Where are you? Please come home." My voice cracks as I hang up and sit at my laptop bringing up a list of hospitals.

There are over a thousand hospitals in the city, and I'm not even halfway through the endless list when light creeps in through the window.

My eyes burn, and fatigue hooks its claws into me. But I don't stop. I can't. Liam is out there somewhere, and I don't know where he is or what happened.

I stretch my legs and go to the kitchen, finding our uneaten meal still on the table. A crusty layer has formed on the fish, and the peas have shrunk into dried-out, green, wrinkly marbles. I discard the food and make a coffee. My heart squeezes in my chest; Liam makes us coffee in the morning.

I keep calling hospitals, taking breaks to call Liam, till my voice is too hoarse and my lids are too heavy and my heart, that's been running overtime, begs me for a break. The panic has nestled itself warmly inside me like a cat on a windowsill and keeps clawing at my insides. I need rest, but I can't close my eyes. Every sound has me jumping and my hands clutch at my phone like a lifeline.

Grabbing the quilt off our second-hand sofa, I wrap it around me. It smells so much like him I feel like cracking. I pace the small space, and my mind keeps running scenarios that scare the shit out of me. I can't fathom a life without Liam. A life where I don't have his voice or can't hear his laughter or can't taste his kisses or feel his arms around me.

I push all the thoughts away and am about to return to my list when my phone trills. My heart leaps and bashes against my rib cage then plummets into the festering pit of my stomach when I see my mother's name flash across the screen. I pick up anyway because, like me, she is tenacious, and she won't stop calling till I do.

"Hi, Mum." Somehow, I hold myself together.

"Evie, you have to come, your dad is having a bad day—" She prattles on, making her problems mine, but today, I can't shoulder more of her burdens.

"I can't."

"You don't have class on Friday morning, you can come help your dad for a few hours." She lances me with the blade of guilt, and I stitch up the wound of her words.

"I can't come today."

"Why? That boy?"

Swallowing the lump of emotions that pushes its way up my throat, I draw in a long breath, sealing my anger inside. "Liam didn't come home last night. Something's happened."

"Probably ran off with some girl."

"Mum!"

"Evangeline, you know I love you, and part of loving someone is telling them the truth. The sooner you face the reality that he is a no-good waste of—"

I hang up. Spears of anxiety and anger skewer my chest. There are so many unknowns, so many questions that swirl through me, and all I need is Liam.

As the day moves on, details become less clear; more phone calls, more silence, more worry until at some point I fall into a fitful broken sleep where Liam holds me in his arms and promises everything will be okay before he dissipates into thin air leaving nothing behind.

T he first week is a blur. I check every homeless shelter and drive into every hospital in town, just in case, but no one has heard of Liam Morrison. He hasn't shown up at work, and the slew of Facebook messages I've sent him remain unread, then vanish as does his profile. Food and sleep become foreign concepts reserved for those who have peace.

The drive down to Blue Haven feels like an out-of-body experience. I've travelled this road so many times I could have driven it with my eyes closed, and yet the closer I get, the more my empty stomach tightens with anticipation and nervousness. My clay hands slip off the steering wheel and my heartbeat drowns out the radio. I can barely continue by the time I hit the edge of town and see the hotel that used to be nothing but a skeleton that hid all our secrets in its unfinished closets.

I keep going. I can't stop till I park my car outside his house. The place he'd lived in all his life till he left his father and sister behind to come and live with me. The house is at the top of a cliff, on the other edge of town, almost inaccessible. His own secret slice of paradise. Someone had carved stairs into the cliff face, and there was a time when we would slip down there in the late afternoons, and I'd sit on the tiny, secluded beach while he surfed till his sister's voice would drift from somewhere above us and call us in for dinner.

I think that I run up to the front door, but really, it's more like I'm floating outside my body. I see myself knocking frantically at the whitewashed door with the crack slicing it all the way down just slightly off centre. I knock till my knuckles ache and my fists burn and my palms can't take the battering. When there is nothing but silence and emptiness, I creep around the property, like a stalker, peering into windows. There is no movement anywhere. Even the garage stands empty. There are no cars, no signs of life.

Abandoned.

Like me.

I retreat to my car and wait.

I don't dare leave or close my eyes, not even for a second. What if I blink and I miss him?

What if...

I had so many of those in the early days, but like so many other questions, I never got my answers.

I sit in the car till the sun sinks beyond the cliff and well into the night. I startle awake sometime later and wonder what woke me. It's well after two a.m. but I don't care as I go knocking at the front door, too tired to notice all the lights still out, all the cars gone. When all I get for my trouble is an aching hand and more silence, I get back in my car and tear off into the darkness.

Two weeks after his disappearance there was still no sign of him. He'd just vanished. Here one day, gone the next. The police promised to help me look, but the look in their eyes as they left my apartment assured me they wouldn't waste their time. They kept asking me if he was seeing someone else, if he had any reason to leave. They wanted access to his bank accounts that were all suddenly empty. They kept telling me that they usually find 84% of missing people and there was hope, or at least answers at the end of my tunnel. Their words gave me a renewed energy.

I kept searching because there was nothing else to do. Obsession possessed me like a demon, and I'd spend every waking hour searching, driven by hope and passion. There were so many places to search and so many posters to hang up and so many hours in the day to fill up without him. If I stopped for only a minute, the pain would flood me, and worry would eat at me, and desperation would claw at my feet and beg for me to collapse and wail alongside it. So, I didn't. I stayed positive despite all the warring feelings inside me. I didn't stop, even when the nurses at the reception desks gave me pitiful looks and when the managers running the homeless shelters asked me if I needed a meal or a place to rest. I didn't stop. I couldn't. I couldn't accept the truth. He'd left and he wasn't coming back.

Three weeks later when I call the cops back, they tell me they have nothing new and that maybe it is time to accept that some people just don't want to be found. They still promise me they'll keep doing their job and keep looking. Pretty sure the officer uses the term 'keeping his ear to the ground'. When I hang up, I feel the last of my hope leaking out of me and I fall onto my bed where I stay and stay and stay.

Everything hurts. My body feels heavy, so all I do is lie down and hide under the blanket. It's been too many weeks and his smell is starting to fade away, skewering me with fear that just like him, it will one day vanish altogether.

My heartbreak feels like shattered glass. The day he didn't come back the first crack appeared, barely the length of a hairpin, but as time dripped away, the crack grew and accelerated into a spiderweb before imploding. The shattering of my heart was instantaneous, vicious and agonizing, and it smashed into a million glittering fragments which scattered across my body, slicing me from the inside. As the initial pain subsided, the shards of what was left behind sliced into me slowly as I tried to gather them and glue myself back together. Every laceration ran deep, each a scarring memory.

<hr>

My mother lets herself in like she owns the place and, as usual, her face twists in the way that it does, like she's smelling something foul. Maybe she is. I don't remember the last time I showered, and the few cups I've used for coffee sit unwashed at the edge of the basin.

"You look like death just spat you out."

I feel it too. I curl into a tighter ball on the bed and try to shut her out, her and the rest of the world. She has no idea of the void he's left behind. The empty long nights when I long to hear his voice. Feel his touch. My days are full of solitude, and I hate everyone. I hate that they smile and walk and enjoy the sunshine. I often wonder how I'll ever fill the growing emptiness.

"When was the last time you ate something?" Her annoying questions pull me out of my thoughts.

I ignore her grating voice. I wish she'd just leave me

alone.

The blanket whips off me by force, and I clutch at empty air, faced with my mother's scowl. She doesn't look sad or concerned, just disappointed. Her indifference stabs at my already tattered heart. "It's time to get up, Evie, it's time to stop this nonsense. This boy you're crying over, he's just a teenage crush, and all these feelings you think you have will pass."

Maybe I don't want them to pass.

She doesn't relent in her badgering; not till she gets me in a shower and watches me push the meal that she brought around the plate. I chew two mouthfuls before my body protests the intrusion and I shove the plate away, getting up. I want to go back to sleep, but she won't let me. Instead, we go for a walk. And it's excruciating. Everything around me reminds me of him. The streets, the corner shop where we'd buy ice cream on Sunday mornings, the fucking brick wall that he kissed me against one time. And then there is everything else. Everything I see that I want to share with him. The things I think he'd laugh at or appreciate. These feelings I have, I want to tell him everything, but every time I turn around, he's not there. When Liam vanished, he didn't just disappear, he stole my joy. He took happiness away. He stole all the colours, leaving behind only grey.

"I think you should move back in with your dad and me."

When I don't answer she keeps going.

"You can help around the house instead of sitting at home all day. Now you've deferred your studies for six months, you have plenty of free time."

"I'm not moving out." My voice sounds foreign even to me; hoarse and lame and empty.

She gives me a long look before continuing, "Well your dad and I aren't going to help pay the rent on that place. You know how much your dad costs every month." Of course I do, she throws it in my face every chance she gets. "How do you intend to keep it?"

I clear my throat. "I'll get a job."

"You used to have goals and dreams. You'll let them all be swallowed up by this boy?" When I say nothing, she scoffs and remains blissfully silent as she drags me into the grocery shop and fills a basket with toiletries and ready-made meals.

We walk back in silence, and she potters around, putting the food away and making a point of showing me the soap and shampoo she's just purchased. Apparently, it's the same one she uses and it smells great. When she leaves, I pour it down the sink. I don't want her smell contaminating our flat and covering up the lingering few nuances left by Liam.

Her visit did nothing for my mood, but it did light a fire under my arse. She is right about one thing; if I don't get work, I'll have to give up the flat, and the thought cuts right through me. I make myself a fresh cup of coffee and sit down at my laptop. Half an hour later I have a dozen potential jobs to apply for.

***

Summer turns into autumn, autumn turns to winter, and winter turns to spring.

I stroke Rabbit as he purrs under my touch before jumping off the chair and threading himself between my legs. Doctor Marshall said I should get a pet to keep me company and keep me busy. I'm sure she meant a dog, but that would mean leaving the house for walks, and I couldn't leave. What if Liam came back? I settled on a rabbit, but they didn't have any at the pet store, so I picked a cat instead. My mother has questioned my name choice. I think it irks her and that alone makes him worth keeping around because her annoyance makes me smile. I scratch the back of his ears, and he gifts me with a loud purr before he stalks off to his food bowl.

I adjust my uniform, taking one last look at the mirror before heading out. The dark blue circles under my eyes have faded slightly, and my face has regained most of its colour and some of its roundness. I look less like the living dead and more like someone who grapples with an eating disorder. Doctor Marshall said it's a process, that it will get better. I choose to believe her, while still clinging to my doubts.

The job at the cafe isn't the realisation of a lifelong dream, but it pays enough for me to keep the flat. But more so, it fills my days. I'm busy making coffees and sandwiches, I clean tables and wash dishes, and it helps. Over the past few months, I've noticed myself reacting less to the sound of the bell at the door. My heart doesn't smash against my spine each time someone walks in and I study their face in hopeful desperation. It's not him.

It's never him.

After a while, the sharp pain begins to fade and, in its place, everything I look at is stained with longing instead.

Tracey has been amazing. She owns the cafe and gave me the job despite me looking like I'd climbed out of a grave the day I came to apply for it. Her empathetic and caring nature was nurturing. She's allowed me my time to grieve, never once asking me if I was still going on about 'that boy'. She never once put a ticking clock on how long I was allowed to wallow in my misery or made me feel that the great epic love I felt for Liam was nothing more than a romanticised teenage crush. She hugged me in the storeroom and told me to sit till my tears dried. She told me to take a sandwich home at the end of every shift, and she bought Rabbit cat food. Not once did she tell me it will be okay and I'll move on. She just let me be. I appreciated that more than anything else.

Yesterday I was distracted enough that I didn't think about him for two whole hours. Until I did. I've noticed I've been able to do that now. Document the passage of time without him. I don't know if it means I'm accepting things. Though on very dark days I find myself wishing that I knew he was dead. I find no comfort in the thought or in the notion, but at least then I'll have closure. I'll have answers. I'll have... something.

My mother has been at me again. School starts in a few weeks, and I'll have to let the job go. The prospect of having to leave the flat looms over me like a thundering black cloud. Doctor Marshall thinks moving in with my mum and going back to school is a good idea—I think she needs her head examined.

Life has taken on a routine. I get up and go to work, end my shift and get back home where I curl into our bed and glare at the door, waiting, always waiting. Rabbit curls up by my body, and I still seek to find Liam's smell on anything, but my tears have washed him away. Doctor Marshall keeps telling me I should make new friends, get out more, but I can't—not just yet. Not while there's still hope Liam will walk through the door.

Tracey paid me an extra month's wage. She didn't have to, but she told me she wanted me to use the money for something fun. Fun. I don't remember what that feels like anymore. I spent too long packing up our small apartment, shedding tears over every T-shirt and pair of jeans I threw into a box. Packing away our memories. The poetry book he read to me before bed, his toothbrush, the snow globe he bought from the Blue Haven souvenir shop.

Moving back into my mother's house with my tail tucked between my legs is like walking into a mausoleum. After living in our warm apartment for so long, these bleak white walls and ramps around every corner drive a wedge into my soul. The house smells sterile like impending death—my father's.

Still, I skulk into my old room. In true fashion, my mother has redecorated it in her 'modern' style, rendering everything white and lifeless. She likes to call it a clean look, but it just feels barren.

School resumes, and I have no choice but to return to the land of the living. Despite her sharp tongue and useless hurtful remarks, I know my mother loves me—somewhere. She drives me to campus every day, ensuring I have lunch, and she drills me about my classes. I don't think she particularly cares about medical terms to describe the human body or its movements, I just think she is making sure I actually attend class.

Over time I settle into a new routine. One that involves school and looking after my father, who is more like a ghost living in her home. But it doesn't matter how much time passes, it hasn't healed anything—not like they say it will in all the songs but rather, it diluted everything—pain, memories, perceptions. It takes time but my heart rebuilds—but it never feels the same—it sits lopsided in my chest, never really beating in the same way.

I met Trent in my third year of Uni. He was studying to be an actuary. He was reserved and quiet. Our story wasn't a romantic one. No fireworks or marching bands. But love is sometimes silent; it's calm and beautiful. He was reliable, solid, constant. Like a river. He never ran dry. He was a great provider, a source of comfort, and he always let me hold the remote.

After the first time he made love to me I locked myself in the bathroom and cried, despite telling myself I had moved on and that I was okay—I wasn't. Liam's hold was too strong, unbreakable. My stomach cramped and vomit crawled up my throat as I admonished myself for cheating on him. Of course, it made no sense, he was gone, and I was with Trent. Trent who was sweet and caring and lovely, but he wasn't Liam. Liam was gone, but I hadn't let him go. I just didn't know how to.

Maybe a part of me, that huge pathetic part that kept hoping, didn't want to hurt Liam, to let him down. Everyone has let him down, but not me. I was the girl who was going to stick around. I wasn't going anywhere... until I did.

When Trent got his diagnosis, he was stoic. Like I knew he would be. He reassured me like he'd always done and promised that I'd be okay after he was gone. Till the very end, he was predictable, reliable and solid. Till he was nothing more than a gaunt corpse and a collection of bitter-sweet memories.

I cried for a solid week. I cried while the funeral director assured me everything would be taken care of. I cried when they put him in the ground. I cried when I walked into our empty bedroom and smelt him everywhere. I cried when I held the damn remote.

The truth is, I wasn't lamenting our love. I didn't miss him in that deep endless way I still sometimes ache for Liam. I missed his companionship and his presence but not much else. That realisation stabs at me. Or maybe it's the renewed thoughts of Liam. A name I've buried so far down, the mere thought of it evokes an avalanche of fresh pain that has nothing to do with my recent loss and everything to do with an alternate life I never got to have.

"You look awful, dear," she says as she places her bag on the counter and makes a beeline for the coffee machine.

"Thanks, Mum." She's always had a way with words. Not good ones but words, nonetheless.

"You should go down to Blue Haven. Have a break. You were always happy there." She's oblivious to the knife she just twisted in my already weeping heart.

"I don't think so." I haven't been to a beach in over ten years. The idea of it makes my skin itch and my chest squeeze. My eyes water again and my mum sighs. The aroma of her steaming coffee wafts through the dim kitchen.

"Just go to the property. Take a few days to yourself. Regroup."

The property. I hate when she calls it that. She's taken Grandad's house and ripped its insides out, erasing its small-town charm and any signs that we ever spent any time there. She painted over the height chart in the kitchen and ripped away the shed in the back that housed the fishing gear. She wiped away our childhood smells and covered it up with paint thinners and fake backsplash.

"I'm fine," I say and watch as she potters around my kitchen putting away food I won't eat and setting the dirty dishes in my overloaded dishwasher. She turns it on, and the chugging drowns away a little of our silence. She'll be back tomorrow to put the clean dishes away.

"Trent has been gone for a month. You need to start moving forward."

The words come easily to her; she's never experienced this kind of loss.

"I'll think about it." I won't.

"You won't."

I shrug, not knowing what else there is to say.

"Moping around here won't bring him back."

"Mum."

"No. I'm not going to sit back and watch you throw your life away. He's gone, you're not. Life is for the living."

"I know."

"Good, then it's settled. The property will be vacant for the next week. Michael will have a key for you."

I nod knowing there is no point in arguing. If I do, she might offer to drive me down there herself and that would be a disaster all on its own.

She downs the rest of her coffee, probably scalding her throat in the process, but she doesn't flinch as she rinses the cup and puts it on the dish rack to dry. "I'll see you when you get back."

She comes around the counter for an awkward hug before she breezes out the door as if all this death and desperation might stink up her clothes. I watch her drive away before I breathe again.

There is still too much left of the day, and the hot summer sun keeps threatening to push its way in through my drawn curtains.

I tiptoe up the stairs. I'm not really sure why; I can't wake the dead even if I tried, but this house feels more like a mausoleum than a home, and the silence here feels deep and ancient and all too familiar.

In our room I stare at the walk-in closet, the door shut. It's white and embossed with a decorative rectangular frame. I've often imagined what it would feel like if Trent fucked me against it. He never did. He was too reliable, too stable; just like that door. And though he was a kind lover, he didn't understand passion. I never burned for him, never ached for his touch, never missed it like the dry earth that demands the rain. He always made sure I came, always a practised perfect lash of his tongue or rolling of his thumb over my clit. Always in our bed just before bedtime, always after the late news bulletin. It was never romantic, just a release. It was always just nice and soft and safe.

I sigh and reach under my bed, grabbing my rucksack. It's been stuffed down there for years. It smells of disuse and abandonment. Trent wanted us to use the suitcases, the ones he bought with his adult money from his adult job; the one that bought us this house and afforded us the life we lived. But the bag reminds me of a past I never really let go of, of a girl that went looking for her future and came home to find a new one.

I stuff a few things into it—a handful of shirts and shorts, a bikini I don't plan on wearing, and a few other bits. I'm not paying as much attention as I should. Trent's side of the closet is just as he left it. Meticulous. My eyes drift over the collection of suits and shoes, the ties all hanging up like a limp rainbow. I step out—I'll deal with this later.

I sink onto the bed and tears sting my eyes. Trent and his stupid perfect plans have left me alone to face the world, and the reality is, that my heart is remembering an older pain, a much sadder and deep-seated pain I thought I'd buried. Trent's loss is dredging up the past, and I don't want to remember the shattered girl I was back then.

I drag in a long breath and push the rising tide back down then crawl under the blanket. Rabbit jumps onto the bed and nestles himself along the curve of my back, just letting me know he is there. I scratch the back of his ear before pulling the blanket over my head. If I sleep, I can pretend none of this exists, that this life belongs to someone else and maybe, just maybe, this pain will belong to someone else.

The single-lane road is now a two-lane motorway. The idyllic scenery that once was part of the anticipation as we left the city is all but gone, replaced by a treacherous tar serpent full of noisy cars that look like scuttling beetles as they zoom by me. Still, there is a familiarity in the way the road meanders and the houses fall away and concrete gives way to nature. Rabbit sits in his box and reminds me of his presence every few kilometres. I keep lying to him and telling him we are almost there. I think he believes me.

As I pull into Blue Haven, the glaring differences slap me in the face. It seems the values of the older generation did not pump in the veins of their children, and greed and exploitation of seaside properties became the norm. The old skeleton hotel has been built, refurbished and modernised. It overflows with guests who no doubt will flood the beautiful sand bar this place has to offer. Homes have been turned into B&Bs and a string of new fish and chip shops and ice creameries line the once quiet main street. Capitalism always wins. It's a little melancholy, but I can't blame people for trying to earn more while working less.

I stop outside the grocery shop that also doubles as the town's post office. Like the rest of the place, it's lost its seaside charm and doubled in size. Mr. Daily must be happy; he's as much an institution here as the ocean, and I find him behind the counter serving a crew of teenagers who think they look cool with their pants hanging halfway up their arses and their ice creams melting on their hands. I cringe thinking of my own teenage days, that time when you're not a kid anymore and trying to be an adult having no real idea what that really means or who you are.

They depart in a bout of laughter, and Mr. Daily spots me. His crystal-clear blue eyes fall on me and his face beams in a beautiful smile. "Evangeline Miller, is that you?"

I can't help but smile back at the old man. His thick white hair springs around his head in a haphazard way as if it's been brushed by the wind. "Yes. Well, it's Walker now."

I get closer to the counter, and his smile fades a little. "I heard about Trent. I'm sorry for your loss."

Everyone always is. "Thank you, Mr. Daily." My smile thins. "Mum said you'd have the key for me?"

"I sure do, and it's Michael; we're too old for niceties." He opens a cupboard door full of jangling keys and finds the one I need. "It sure is good to see your face after so many years." He hands me my key.

If he wants me to say that it's good to be back or that I missed this place, I won't. "Thanks."

"Don't hesitate to call me if you need anything. I'll drive it out to you myself."

"Thanks, Mr. Daily, I'm sure I'll be fine."

He tips his head, and the warmth returns to his face even if the pity doesn't leave his eyes. "Welcome back."

I get out of the shop and back into mye car, my breath suddenly short and my palms clammy. Why the hell did I come back here? Rabbit mewls impatiently, like he agrees. I scan the street; it's full of revellers and tourists buying souvenirs. It eases my mind, this place, like this. It's almost foreign. I draw in a few settling breaths before I start the car and drive the last stretch to the house.

I pull into the driveway and look at the stairs leading up to the porch. Mum had everything repainted white and crisp, and the sun jumps off the banister, forcing my eyes to narrow even with my sunglasses. My heart somersaults in my chest—there are so many memories living inside me and they all want to run out of me all at once. I push them down knowing I have an entire weekend to deal with all my ghosts, new and old, before I leave this place behind. For good.

The key slots easily into the door and I push it open. The house, as expected, feels nothing like it used to. My mother has ripped out its soul and turned it into a version of herself. Cold and uninviting.

Setting Rabbit's box on the floor, I leave it open and allow him time to slink out and explore at his leisure. I can't blame him for wanting to hide inside his enclosure; maybe he feels safer there. I drop my bag onto the impeccable marble top of the kitchen island and take a look around. I could be anywhere, except that a few things haven't changed. Not the way that I feel, not the way the air tastes or smells, not the lapping waves that chase each other from across the road.

I make a cup of coffee and sit by the window watching the ocean. My stomach churns with the waves. I sit in my lonely command post near the edge of the world, my mind swinging back and forth to the empty spaces left behind; a place between memory and desire. Time ticks by. The waves keep lapping and my coffee turns cold.

There are many kinds of sadness. There's a sadness that's like a breeze, it's a passing thought that brushes over you. You shiver but only for a moment before you find warmth again. But then there is the sadness that stains your soul, and no matter how hard you try to clean it, it sticks to you like melted gum on the bottom of a shoe. This is the sadness you carry with you everywhere. It's haunting and creeps up at the most unexpected moments. There's no rhyme or reason to it being there, and yet so many little things let it tug at you.

It is a bottomless pool that once you've waded into, all you can do is tread water and hope you don't get sucked under. This is the pain I carry with me. I wallow in it as I sit on my mother's plush new couch and contemplate life alone.

This was never the plan. To be 33 and a widow. I'm almost grateful now we didn't have any children. It's not that we didn't want them, it's that we both worked on our careers and time sort of slipped away. And maybe secretly in my heart of hearts, I can admit that I never wanted them to be Trent's. After so long of picturing what my kids would look like with Liam's wild hair and cheeky smiles, anything else would have felt like settling, and no child should feel like that.

I set aside my unfinished coffee and allow the lethargy to wrap itself around me. Sorrow sucks away so much energy.

I slide the curtains shut keeping the sunshine and life out and turn towards the corridor. Sleep will make everything better.

***

I wake to the roll of thunder and a cool darkness that veils the town. These late afternoon summer storms are not unusual. Rabbit's ears perk up and he eyes the room nervously. I run my fingers along his soft coat. "Shhhh, it's just a storm."

Thunderstorms were always my favourite part of summer. Their raw, violent power is exhilarating. The way the lightning is like an organic flash of a camera that will never have its pictures developed. The way the rain falls heavily; I always felt like I should see through it—because water is clear after all—but I couldn't. The way the clouds made the world grey, and the way they crashed Liam into my arms.

I lie in my bed listening listlessly to the symphony of raindrops and the fingertips of the trees tapping on my windowpane. My thoughts keep drifting back to Liam.

The clouds rumble across the sky and hide the sunshine like a fluffy grey blanket. The air is thick with humidity, and Liam runs out of the water, his board tucked under his arm. He's wearing a smile that belongs in a fashion magazine and his wet hair whips around in a frenzy as he shakes water and sand from it. I could have watched Liam like that for an eternity, carefree and happy.

A crash of lightning has me jumping, and he throws his board down, pulling me into his arms.

"Afraid of a little rain?" he teases as the first heavy drops fall from the sky.

"I'm afraid of nothing." I push his chest, but he just clings to me tighter, as if maybe I'm the one comforting him. My heart chugs in my chest as warmth passes between us. This boy who has been my best friend has been affecting me in ways a friend shouldn't, and yet for the last two years, each time I see him my entire body comes to life and all my thoughts concentrate into one single word. Liam.

He's yet to release me, and the thundering of my heart threatens to drown out the lashing storm. His hazel eyes sparkle as they look into mine, and rivulets slink along his face and drip down his chin onto his bare torso.

I want to tell him that we should be heading back up to his house, that we should get out of the blistering wind that has started turning the air cold, that my mum will be furious when I arrive soaked and dishevelled, but I don't. Instead, I revel in the feel of his arms around me and his body along my own. In the way his eyes look at me like they are seeing more than just my face, but all my secret desires and needs for him.

I can't help it. My hands slink slowly up his back, and I push up on my tip toes before I plaster a quick kiss on his lips.

His eyes grow big as he stares down at me, and I feel the sting of heat burn across my chest and face, searing the tips of my ears. He says nothing, just a long lingering look that has me doubting everything and wishing I hadn't just done what I did. I try to pull away, but his arms tighten around me in resistance, between us only heat and silence before his head tips down and his lips crash hard into mine, and Liam Morrison kisses me.

Our lips move and dance in a frenzy, uncertain and volatile, learning one another for the first time, but it's when his tongue breaches the seam of my lips and searches for mine that he washes away any unseen pain, doubt, or angst. I know then, in that moment, that Liam Morrison is mine.

For the time our lips were locked together in that rush of rain, the world itself ceased to exist as we rebelled against the elements and found one another. When Liam pulls away, his face is a picture of ecstasy as he tips his head up towards the sky that promises more rain, and begins to laugh.

Forked lightning slices the sky and pulls me from the memory, and I shake my head trying to clear it. Coming back was a terrible idea. I should have called Dr. Marshall; she would have talked Mum out of it. She would have made me see sense.

Instead, I'm here waiting for old memories to fade into the realm of distant memory, but they won't. They stubbornly linger in the forefront of my consciousness like an unwanted guest. Unwanted but inevitable.

I'm ripped away from my thoughts and my bed by a strange sensation, like thunder rumbling inside my body. A sudden deafening crack roars through the house, making it shake and tremble. Rabbit jumps out of my arms and scampers away. There's a few seconds of silence before I hear the tearing, like screaming wood. I can almost feel it reverberate through me. It's followed by a gust of rushing water, like the house has been transported to the edge of a waterfall. I throw the duvet off and bolt upright, running through the door to find water cascading down the ceiling fan and trickling along the floor in a turbulent river.

I look up to see branches; they pierce the roof where rain

falls carelessly into the house. I run to the power board and switch it off before running outside. The water pelts my face and body, and my clothes stick to me like a child's unfinished papier-mâché, getting heavier by the minute as they soak up more water.

The neighbour's tree has snapped off at the base and is now being supported by the house, but I can't tell the full extent of the damage and won't be able to till the tree is removed.

I look up into the grey sky as it mocks me, and the rain keeps battering my face, saturating my hair that now sticks to my face, and I want to scream. I want to cry out into the heavens. I want my voice to soar and for answers to come, but I don't.

I walk back into the house leaving behind puddles for footprints as I find my phone. The afternoon storm is already ebbing, and soon the sun will come out and erase any trace that it ever existed.

I sit and stare at the screen. The one benefit of being here is distance from her, and yet, somehow, this storm has managed to drag her back into my life.

I sigh and dial.

"What's wrong?" She's already on alert and ready to pounce. She's like that, my mum, always expecting the worst. Sometimes I wonder if it's some kind of defence mechanism for her sanity; just makes getting bad news easier.

"Nothing," I lie, or at least try to cushion the blow. "Well…"

"What is it, Evangeline?" My name feels so ironic just now.

"A tree fell on the house. There's some damage to the roof, but it's hard to tell what else."

"Did you switch off the electricity?"

"Yes." My fingers grip the bridge of my nose. "I was in the house when it happened. I'm fine, thanks for asking."

"Well clearly you are, you're calling me, aren't you? The electricity? Did you switch it off?"

"Yes, obviously."

"Well, nothing is really obvious with you."

I grit my teeth and breathe out the annoyance building inside me. "Who do you want me to call to fix this?"

"I'll call Michael. He has the name of the builder who redid the house."

"I can—"

"I said I'll do it."

"Okay." My head falls back, and I look at the ceiling. A sharp branch snapped in half pokes through the new hole. A single green leaf still clinging on.

"Stay put, someone will come soon."

"What if the roof collapses and the house falls on my head?"

"Your dramatics are unnecessary." She huffs and hangs up on me.

Thanks, Mum.

I set my phone on the kitchen counter and get back to the bedroom. I peel the wet clothes from my body and throw them on the floor in defiance. She makes me feel like a toddler, and just like a child, guilt and shame gnaws at my inside when I see the puddle forming on the beautifully polished wooden floor. I gather the clothes and discard them in the bath. Somehow wetting her floor is a hollow victory.

I find Rabbit. He's hiding under the blanket, and I gather him in my arms, stroking his delicate fur. "It's okay, boy, just a little storm." There's no point explaining to a cat the intricacies of a tree through the roof. But I do anyway; he is a good listener.

I set him back down and dry the puddle my clothes left on the floor. I search for a stain, lying to myself that I'm not relieved I don't find one.

By the time I am dressed and dry, the storm has vanished leaving behind a dazzling blue sky.

There's a knock on the door.

Michael has sent the builder already. Mum has probably been in his ear about how I'm struggling and can't look after myself. They probably had a long chat about 'what happened the *first* time.'

I tuck the wet strands of my hair behind my ears and make my way through the corridor, dodging puddles I probably should have wiped away.

When I open the door, there's a man looking over his shoulder at someone following in his wake. He's holding an old-fashioned toolbox and his tattooed arm cords from the weight.

"Hello?" I try to grab his attention, and he turns to face me. The blood runs cold in my veins.

Fourteen years have changed him, but not enough that I don't recognise him instantly and my knees want to buckle.

Seeing Liam again drains all the oxygen from my lungs. I am sucked back under water and reduced to the beating of my aching heart where there is no air or light or reason, just him. Or the ashes of what he left behind after he left me burning.

"Liam?" His name is barely a whisper that passes my lips as my body quakes with the shock.

His eyes latch onto mine, and recognition passes over his features. He opens his mouth to say something, but his companion comes bursting from behind him. "Dad, is this going to take long? I wanted to go to the cinema with Julie later."

Dad? Liam is alive and he has a kid? I got a cat, and he

got a fucking daughter?

I can't bring myself to look at her as my eyes remain glued on Liam's. He glares at me. There's something in his eyes I can't read. Hate? Fear? Anger?

The girl comes from behind him, she's chewing on a stick of gum and is wearing faded paint-stained jeans and a navy-blue T-shirt. She can't be more than 14, and when I look at her face I can see a resemblance to Liam. She has his eyes.

"Dad?" she whines again, and he turns to her as she stops and looks over me.

My stomach rolls and tumbles. I'm going to be sick.

Liam still says nothing. He stands there like a stone statue, his eyes back on my face.

My heart explodes in my chest instead of beating, and I want to cry, and scream, and throw myself at him, to touch his face and feel if he's real, and I want to do it all at once, but my feet are glued to the floor and the bile keeps rising in my throat.

"Dad?" the girl's tone is a little more wary as her gaze swings between us.

"Let's go," he growls at the girl and turns to leave. "Nothing we can do here till they clear that away." He tips his head to the branches poking through the ceiling, and the girl's eyes follow his gesture.

"Aww, but I need the pocket money from this job," she calls after him, but he's already opening the door to his truck and slamming it shut behind him.

She turns back to me, shrugs and mumbles an apology before joining him in the truck. He speeds off before she has a chance to close the door.

I watch the empty street, and my knees finally buckle before I double over, vomiting all over the floor.

That's definitely going to stain.

LIAM

My heart keeps jack-knifing in my chest, and no matter how hard I try, my breaths will not settle down. Nessa keeps giving me worried side glances, and after her third 'are you okay' that I've ignored, she's keeping quiet and her eyes on her phone.

She just took me by surprise, that's all. I never expected to see her again. Not after the last time. I bite down on my lip, hard enough to draw blood. I release it when a trickle of metallic taste coats my tongue.

She looks different again, older, tired, way too skinny, and yet perfectly stunning. Though, as she looked at my face, she looked as though she'd just been punched. I can't blame her. I can't blame her for anything, but seeing her here... Fuck. She shouldn't be here. She shouldn't be anywhere near me. Or maybe it's the other way around?

Because the minute I saw her, every unresolved feeling, every memory, every regret I have been carrying with me came crashing inside me all at once, and I had to get away because it was the only way I could stop myself from pinning Evie down and asking her what the fuck she was doing in Blue Haven, and a thousand other questions that demanded answers.

I drive too fast and park like an idiot, tyres screeching and the whole car jerking as I plant my feet on the brakes too heavily.

"What the hell, Dad?"

Shit. "I'm sorry."

"Are you okay?"

No. I'm the furthest away from okay I've been in a long time and seconds away from losing my mind. "Yeah, I'm fine. Here." I take out my wallet and hand her a few notes. "Your pay for today. Go to Julie."

"Really?" She beams up at me, and despite my entire body feeling knotted and tight, I manage a thin smile.

"Make sure you call me if you need a ride back."

She nods but is already running into the house, to change no doubt, her nose in her phone, probably letting her friend know she is on her way. I let out a deep breath. I need the house to myself. I need a fucking drink.

I call Michael first and let him know there's nothing I can do till the tree has been removed. He knew that, so a part of me wonders why the hell he sent me over there to begin with. My history with Evie is not a mystery in this town, and everyone knows he holds the keys to all the B&Bs in town. Whatever fucking game he is playing rubs me the wrong fucking way. He might be an old man, but that doesn't stop my sudden urge to have a violent encounter with him in a dark corner.

"Why the hell did you send me over to the Miller property? You knew there was nothing I could do there, and you knew she was there, didn't you?"

"Evangeline?"

"Yes," I bite out at the old man.

"Didn't think that was a problem. You two used to be good friends, and she's going through a rough time."

"A tree falling through a house isn't a rough time."

"No, I guess not, but losing a husband is."

The air falls out of my lungs. Her husband is dead. Part of me feels like I'm breathing a sigh of relief. I don't even feel guilty about it. "I'm sure she has enough friends. Call me when the tree has been removed."

I hang up because my body is shaking, and I keep ignoring the stir of emotions that threatens to send me spiralling.

Nessa bursts from the house. She's wearing makeup again and looks too old in a young body. I want her to wipe that shit off and to dress like the little girl that she is, even though she isn't really one and hasn't been for a while now. There is too much going on inside of me to pick a fight; we will both lose if I do.

I plant a kiss on the top of her head. "Have fun, and be safe."

She rolls her eyes at me and walks out of the driveway. Julie's house is at the end of the street. I'm not worried. Well, no more than usual.

When she is finally gone, I barge into the house and go for the fridge. Beer sounds like the best idea I've had all morning. Erase all my issues with alcohol. I've never really had that option before, not when Nessa was young, not when she needed me to look after her, but she's older now and capable, and I just need something to take the edge off.

I reach for the bottle and set it back, before turning to the liquor cabinet instead. Beer won't do what I need it to do. I grab the bottle of whiskey and unscrew the cap before taking a long swig. The alcohol burns everything inside me. It's not a good burn, but I don't care as I take another long sip and feel the heat move down my throat and to my belly where the knotted rope inside me tightens, threatening to never untangle. I shrug. Fuck it, with enough alcohol I'll just burn it out.

I fall onto the couch and let my head fall back as the alcohol begins to take effect and the edges start to feel bearable, and my lungs feel like they can breathe again and my heart, well fuck, that bastard is still doing its own thing.

I keep drinking, just once I'm allowed to be irresponsible and stupid and not think about anyone else other than me.

And Evie.

A knot was tangling itself through all my internal organs. I shouldn't have come. It was dangerous and stupid and incredibly selfish of me, but it's been over three years and I fucking miss her. I've never stopped missing her, thinking about her, wondering how she is without me, if she thinks about me or misses me too. The knots tighten and pull me into my core, hunching my shoulders.

Nessa wiggles in her pram and smiles at passers-by while I stare at her parents' house. I have no other starting point, no way of knowing where else she might be. Her social profiles are all set to private, and my fake profile can't see past the few public pictures she has on. She no longer has the two of us set as her profile picture. My heart stuttered the day I saw she changed it. I didn't want her moving on, even though she deserved to.

My feet feel cemented to the ground as I keep staring at the house. After spending all those hours on the bus and walking across town, these last few steps should feel the easiest and yet, I can't seem to take them.

Nessa gets restless and starts to fight the belts of the pram. I fall on one knee and smile at the beautiful baby girl who has me wrapped so tightly around her tiny finger. "Just a little longer," I say as I search through the bag, produce a small bag of chips and hand it to her. She grabs it in her chubby hands and squeals in delight just as the door of the house I had been staring at cracks open.

Three people walk out. My breaths are uneven and my chest feels heavy, as though a weight has been pressed against it, as I recognise the back of Evie's head. She's hugging her mother who is telling her how good it was to see her. I know Evie doesn't feel the same; she's never really happy to see her mum, given the tumultuous relationship they have.

When they turn around, my breath leaves me. It's Evie. She looks good. Her hair has gotten longer, and she wears it loose; she's in a pair of short jeans and has a black singlet on that shows off her shape. She's already changed, transformed, the last of her adolescent body vanished and is swallowed up by that of a curvier sexier woman. My hands itch to touch her, wrap themselves around her waist and pull her close, till I can kiss her, but just as I'm about to stand, the man, who I've mostly forgotten about or chosen to ignore, wraps his hand around her shoulder. They take the porch steps two at a time, and he whispers something into her ear, making her laugh.

I freeze. Every part of me turns to ice as I watch him lead her away. Of course she's moved on. Why wouldn't she? She is young and beautiful and funny and fucking perfect and coming here was selfish. It was irresponsible and pathetic to think she would wait for me after all this time. He makes her happy, and the thought of someone else doing that stabs at my chest like a thousand blunt swords.

Nessa notices the shift in my mood, and she reaches out for me. I pull her from the pram, and she wraps her small arms around me, melting some of the ice around my heart. Giving it a new reason to beat. To go on. Evie has moved on. I've become the ghost I needed to be when everything went wrong, and now the only thing that matters is this little girl. And she needs me. Evie is fine. Even if I'm not.

I shake the memory away. It was stupid then and it's

stupid now. After that day, I did everything I could to drown her out. During the day I was Nessa's dad; I was attentive and loving and gave her what she needed, even if I couldn't always give her what she wanted. But at night, at night I was a savage broken animal who took his anger and loneliness out on any woman that could stand my alcohol breath and let me fuck her like she was nothing but a hole.

But living like that couldn't last, not when you have a kid to look after, not when you have to get up, even if your head wants to explode and your heart is dead. I could stay reckless and throw away everything I had left in a moment of angry denial, or I could grow up and do what was right for Nessa.

So, I sobered up and got myself qualified, and slowly, over time, I began to feel again. Little moments of joy with Nessa that wound themselves slowly through my veins and thawed out the deep ice that settled inside me. And while I would never be the same, while I could never go back to being careless or purely happy, I could be good. And up until twenty-five minutes ago, I was.

I take another long swig from my whiskey and let the alcohol burn away my pain.

Rabbit meows somewhere in the house, but I can't bring myself to get out of this bed and find him, or feed him, or give him whatever comfort he seeks. I'm engulfed by darkness, the weight of my duvet the only thing keeping me down, keeping me from floating away.

Breathe in.

Breathe out.

I keep sucking in small gulps of air. *Liam is alive.* So why do I feel like dying?

I keep watching the door. Waiting, waiting for him to show up, to walk in, to gift me with one of his beaming smiles and wrap me up in his warm embrace. I keep waiting for him. The clock keeps moving and still I wait and watch and wait like there is nothing else to do. Maybe if I wait long enough, I'll wake up to find him in the bed, right here next to me where he belongs. Maybe if I keep waiting long enough, this pain will melt away like wax succumbing to a flame. Maybe if I wait long enough, he'll love me enough to come back and I can stop waiting. But he doesn't. He doesn't come back, and I keep waiting my life away.

There is pounding at the front door, but I've learned

from experience that if I ignore it long enough it will go away. So I do, and the pounding stops. I lie in the darkness where my thoughts expand and grow as they often do in the dark and the quiet till they threaten to drown my entire world. But in this bubble of darkness, there is no world, only thoughts and memories and so many unfulfilled dreams.

My ringtone cuts through my wallowing, and just like the pounding, I want to ignore it, but I know this ringtone and I know that I can't ignore it. She will just keep ringing till I pick up, and if I don't, inevitably, she'll show up.

My hand slinks under the duvet and into the world and blindly feels for the phone. I grab it and the light blinds my eyes as I pull it back under the blanket and into my dark cocoon.

"Evie?" She sounds annoyed. *There's a surprise.*

"Hi, Mum." I barely recognise my own voice.

"What's wrong?" I recognise her tone and clear my throat. The last thing I need is her showing up thinking I'm not well.

"Nothing, just a tickle, must have been that rain."

She huffs before getting on. "There are men outside the property. They've come to remove the tree. They say they've been knocking..."

"Yeah, I was just about to—"

"Now, about that."

Breathe in.

Breathe out.

"I want you to stay at the property till they finish fixing up the house."

"Mum—"

"I've already spoken to Shelly, she said you can have another week off—"

"You spoke to my boss?" I'm incredulous.

"I was just being pre-emptive; you should learn from me."

"Mum, I don't want—"

"Well, you have to. The property needs fixing and you are already there. You know how hard it is for me to get down there." She digs her dagger of guilt deep into my heart, reminding me yet again in her roundabout way that I wasn't there that night.

"I want to go home."

"What for? I need you there. Someone has to make sure those guys don't steal anything."

"Mum!" The woman astounds me, and not in a good way.

"Evangeline, this is not a punishment, it's an opportunity, use it."

"But—" The line goes dead, cutting off any further argument, and a minute later the pounding resumes.

Whether I like it or not, the world keeps turning, and even if I want to retreat from it, it keeps sucking me back in by force.

***

The shrill whirring of electric saws and hammers keep banging and buzzing inside my head like irritating insects. They asked me to leave, to spend the day away, just in case, but the bed is soft and warm, and with the curtains drawn I can remain in darkness. It's cowardly perhaps, but it feels safe. Here, in my bubble, the rest of the world doesn't exist, and the fact that Liam chose to leave me can't hurt as bad or stab as deep. I can feel my breaths as they blow in and out of my lungs and my pathetic heart chugs sluggishly in my aching chest.

At one point there is a lot of shouting, and the house

groans and creaks and rips and shakes, and fingers of light slide under the door from the giant hole left by the fallen tree that's been viciously ripped from its purchase on my roof; just like the heart in my chest. I wonder if it screamed as they pulled it away. Another ridiculous thought by a silly girl hiding under her blanket instead of facing the world.

Rabbit meows again. He must be hungry. The sunny day has slowly turned into a dusky evening, and the machines stop whirring and silence falls on the house, gripping me with fear. But it is not the quiet I fear, it's what it's going to bring in the morning.

Liam.

LIAM

I jerk awake and my eyes rip open just to fall shut again. Pain radiates in my skull, and my body feels heavy and slow. I blink a few times and lick my chapped lips, my heavy eyelids fighting the light.

Groaning, I sit up, and every part of my body protests the movement. Looking around, I find myself on the small couch, the whiskey bottle nearly empty at my feet and light pouring in from the windows.

I push my palms into my eyes and rub some of the exhaustion away, knowing it will do nothing to relieve the headache that settles more comfortably inside my skull with every passing second.

I reach for my phone, checking the time. I have over fifteen missed calls and two texts from Emma, Julie's mum. Fuck—Nessa. I frantically swipe at my screen and read the message. Emma is reassuring me that Nessa can stay the night and I can pick her up whenever I'm done with the job I had lined up for today. I read over the drunken half-witted messages I left her the night before asking her if Nessa could stay. I don't remember sending them but thank all the gods that she agreed. Then I read over her message again—I can pick Nessa up when I'm done with the job I have lined up for today.

Fuck.

I look over my missed calls. Twelve are from Michael. I guess he wants to talk. One is from Dylan; he must have wanted to catch up for a drink last night. I'll call him back later. The last two are from Olivia; she still doesn't understand the meaning of no strings attached and keeps calling. I guess after fucking her more than three times she now thinks it's a regular thing. Of course, there is nothing wrong with Olivia; she is sexy as fuck, a single mum and willing to do almost anything as long as I make her feel like I care about her for a few hours a week. She is sweet and charming and has a great sense of humour and maybe, just maybe, if Evie hadn't shown up and upended my entire world with a single look, we could have had something. It wouldn't have been fireworks and lightning strikes, but it would have been something...

I head for the shower letting the hot water batter my back and sail down my face. I suck in hot water, washing away the furry layer that coats my teeth. Running my tongue over the roof of my mouth, I blow out a breath and crinkle my nose. I could set fire to a house with it.

I dress and make toast. I'm pretty sure it's all I can handle at this stage, and my body needs something to soak up the alcohol that is still sloshing inside me. As I take my first bite, my phone goes off again. I guess it's time to face the unavoidable.

"Good morning." Michael sounds too loud and too cheery for a Sunday morning.

"What can I do for you?"

"The Miller house needs a quote on the job."

I blow out a breath that could probably still light a cigarette and brush my hands through my wet hair, raining small droplets around me. "I don't think I'm the right guy for the job."

"You practically rebuilt that place."

It's true. I allowed Evie's mum tear away every piece of soul from that house, every little thing that meant anything to Evie and conformed to her emailed plans to turn it into something hollow and empty. Then she tried to talk down my price.

"Let her get someone else."

"Who? One of those big shot builders from the city that built all the hotels around here? You and I both know they will rip her off, do a shoddy job and in three months you'll have to go in and fix their bloody mess."

I hated that he was right, and I hated that he knew just how to get to me. Building something with your hands should be a point of pride, not a place to cut costs and fuck people over.

"Fine," I rumble. "Will the occupant still be there?"

"I believe she's extended her stay until the work is done."

Fucking perfect.

EVIE

I've managed to pull myself together in the same way that you rake together fallen leaves and leave them piled up under a tree. They are a beautifully constructed mess that is held together by sheer willpower and yet entirely vulnerable to the slightest gust of wind. I'll be fine. Even if Liam is a fucking hurricane.

The floor and walls are coloured a light blue as the sun shines over the tarp covering the hole left by the tree, and a light breeze manages to creep in from beneath the plastic sheet that protects the now naked side of the house.

I jerk at the loud banging even though I expect it, and Rabbit jumps off my lap and hides behind the curtain. I draw in a long breath and hesitate for a second. I'd rather hide like Rabbit; we're both cowards. Instead, I walk to the door and swing it open where a version of Liam I'm still getting used to stands and glares at me as if he wishes for me to burst into flames.

We stand there for too long, his angry eyes that used to look at me like I was the only person in the world, now weighed down, heavy and burning holes into me. While I try to recognise some of the boy I knew in his older face. His dark hair peeks from under the cap he wears, and his sharp jaw is covered in a day's worth of growth. He looks exhausted and fucking furious.

"Can I come in?" he finally says, and his voice is deep and scratched as if he's swallowed a load of gravel before coming over.

I step aside, still staring at this apparition, fighting my fingers from reaching out and touching him, making sure he's real. My heart feels heavy in my chest as if it has fallen into the pit of my stomach that just feels hollow, and my gaze follows him as he walks inside.

I follow silently behind him, mesmerised by his shape, by his realness, by the way my heart feels alive and dying all at the same time.

He sets down the toolbox and examines the roof and walls, his eyes expertly roaming over the damage as he scrubs his chin. "I need to get a quote out to your mum." His tone is emotionless and empty and carves a long deep wound inside me.

I nod at his back, still unable to form words.

He swirls around and takes a step towards me. I want to retreat, but I can't move. "I need to get something out of my truck." He scowls at me as his eyes burn.

We step at the same time. I try to get out of his way, and he chooses the same direction as I do. We crash into one another. We try again just to walk into one another for a second time, stumbling around like drunks.

"Would you just get out of the way," he growls at me, and something inside me breaks.

"Why are you acting pissed off when I'm the one who has the right to be angry? You just show up here after you've been gone for years. You just disappeared. No notes, no phone calls. Nothing. You vanished into thin air. And I looked for you. For years I searched. Not wanting to believe the worst. I called every hospital—*for months*—and searched the streets, put up fliers, went to homeless shelters. I drove back here a hundred fucking times, but everyone said you were gone. You were a fucking ghost, and all you left in your wake were endless questions—you just *left me*."

"Evie—" His tone softens, and the fire in his eyes changes from an angry inferno to a slow burn.

"How could you?"

"Evie—"

"No! I mourned you. You died. I carried your ghost for years, asking questions I never thought I'd get the answers to. I wondered why you left, why I was never good enough for you, why I wasn't worth a phone call or a goodbye. What did I do wrong?" I whimper as my voice cracks, and I suck in a broken breath. "All I ever did was love you. I've soaked through my pillow night after night, stopped eating, stopped fucking living—because life without you was..." I gulp for air even though there is none. "It was *nothing*."

"Evie—"

"You have a daughter?!" Though it comes out as a question, we both know it to be fact.

"Nessa is—"

"Nessa?" I whisper her name, and I feel it hack my heart into pieces as nausea takes residence in my belly. He called her Nessa, the name we were going to give our daughter. *Ours.*

His face crumbles, and he opens his mouth to speak, but I can't hear anything he says as I retreat. My legs carry me away from him, as my mind fractures and tries to rebuild itself all at once, tries to be strong, tries to survive another wave of agony, another hurricane of heartbreak, another devastating blow.

I slam the door to the bedroom, shutting him out, shutting everything out. The darkness embraces me as it always does, whispering empty promises of comfort which are only ugly lies, because in the darkness only pain and misery grows, and that bitch loves company.

I throw myself onto the bed and hide under the covers, like a child afraid of a storm. I have survived this storm before; it washed everything away and showed me what was rotten and what I needed to fix. Fourteen years later, I find myself trying to barricade myself from the onslaught of emotion because I don't know if my heart can survive a second battering.

The darkness amplifies everything; the pain, the crushing devastation, and the sound of my breathing. That's what I cling to.

Breathe in.

Breathe out.

I hear footsteps. Heavy, determined footsteps that stop at my door. I keep listening and almost hear his hesitation as he stands on the other side before his fingers wrap themselves around the doorknob and turn it ever so slowly, as if he isn't sure he should be doing it.

The light beneath the door morphs into a triangle that enlarges with every inch he pushes, and I stare at it as my heart smashes in my chest wanting to escape my rib cage.

"Evie?"

His hoarse whisper is broken and thick with emotion. Or maybe that's just my mind playing tricks, wanting to hear things that aren't really there. I can't really tell as his face is cast in shadow, a silhouetted monster at my door.

I don't respond.

He clears his throat as if to make his presence known. "Evie?" he calls louder this time. A flicker of broken voice permeated this one.

"I need you to leave," I say in a voice that doesn't belong

to me. It belongs to someone stronger, better, braver. Someone who isn't cowering in the dark.

"Can we talk?"

I intertwine my trembling fingers and bite down on my wobbling jaw. There was a time I would have chewed off my own right arm just to have the opportunity to speak to him, to tell him every mundane detail of my day knowing he would listen. But now there is nothing but silence. I guess after a while the sadness festered into anger, and that's all I have to hold on to now as he tries to blow away the barricades I have built around my heart.

He takes another step in but says nothing, and I feel his eyes searching the darkness, searching for me. He has no idea what it's like to search.

"Stop." He does and stands like a statue as a profound silence gathers in the room. So heavy I could almost taste it. It tastes like emptiness. "Please." I'm begging now because my strength is dwindling and I'm spiralling. "Please just leave, just go."

"The quote for the house—"

I suck in a breath, knowing I will have to explain any delay to my mother. It's just another conversation I don't want to have.

"Do what you need to do and close the door behind you when you leave."

He hesitates again, just for a second, before I think I see him nod and the door closes behind him, sealing me in the darkness of my makeshift storm shelter. I pull the blanket back over my head and pretend I can't hear him moving around the house.

The back of my head hits the closed door, and I draw in a long breath trying to calm myself, swallowing to curb the emotion that rises inside me. She just dissolved into pain, nothing like the carefree, happy girl I once left behind. Evie reminds me of plexiglass; you can see right through her, every emotion clearly visible with every twitch of her lips and arch of a brow. She is breakable and indestructible all at the same time. No matter what keeps being hurled at her, she shatters and cracks but remains intact, somehow.

I gaze at the flapping tarp above my head, the blue rippling across the walls like a silent sea, before I unglue myself from the door and begin looking at the damage left by the tree.

The damage looks like my insides feel, ripped and torn and crushed in places, yet everything stands. The foundations are still strong, just like I kept them, just like Evie and I used to be. We might be ripped and broken, but our foundations were always strong. If I could only get her to listen.

I walk around the house surveying the damage, and the

more I walk around, the heavier my feet feel, like the anger that simmers to the surface of my skin is cementing me in place. Why the fuck does Evie get to be the one who's pissed off? She says I don't have a right to be, but she left me just as much as I left her. She never showed. She chose to forget me, to move and never look back. She chose to let our fire die. She chose. I didn't get that luxury.

With those thoughts circulating inside me like a vicious tornado, I measure fractured beams and count broken tiles noting down everything I'd need to get this job done and away from this ghost house. I press the pencil too viciously into the paper till I break the tip. Clenching my jaw and running a hand over my face, I let out a frustrated breath.

This isn't going to work.

"You have the okay to start work on the Miller house." His voice is way too fucking cheery for a Monday morning.

"Great," I say unenthusiastically as my stomach clenches and Evie's tormented face comes crashing into my mind. "I'll start work today," I tell Michael through clenched teeth.

"Wonderful, I'll let Mrs Miller know."

"Yeah, about that."

He pauses, and a doorbell chimes in the background. A muted voice carries over the earpiece. "What's the problem?"

"I need Evie—" I clear my throat. "*The occupant*, gone."

"I'm sure you can ask her yourself."

"No. I can't," I say too firmly.

"I see."

"Good." I hang up and put on my best fake smile as

Nessa gets in the car. She doesn't even look at me. A day ago it would have bothered me, now I'm almost happy about raising a teenage daughter.

She barely acknowledges me as I drop her off at school and go to the lumberyard to grab the wood I'll need. By the time I get to the house, it's well after nine, and I have no idea if Michael has relayed my message or not.

Sitting in my truck like an idiot, I watch the house, wondering if Evie has left yet. Her car is still parked outside, but in a town like this, where the beach and the main street are within walking distance, that doesn't mean anything.

I decide to take my chances. Daylight is wasting, and although this is a well-paid gig, I've had to push a few other jobs back to accommodate for the urgency. I knock on the door and wait. I knock for a second time and still, there's no answer.

I find myself letting out a breath I didn't know I was holding and use my spare key to get inside. The tarp flaps above me as if in greeting, and I put my toolbox by the door using it as a stop before I get back to my truck to start offloading.

The stack of wood is heavy, and it slips off my shoulder, crashing to the floor with a heavy thud that vibrates through the wooden floor.

"Fuck," I mumble as I bend over to examine the damage no doubt left on the polished floor, when Evie's bedroom door swings open and her puffy eyes land on mine. Guilt stabs my chest for just a second as I imagine her crying throughout the night, but the shock turns into anger, and she glares at me.

"What the hell are you doing here?"

"It's called work."

"Come back later, it's early."

"It's after nine." She looks at the empty space where the big clock used to hang then back at me. "Michael was meant to call you and tell you to get out."

"Get out?"

"That's not what I meant, just that you shouldn't be here."

She gives me a long cold look. "You're right, I shouldn't be here."

"That's not what I mea—" But she's already slammed her bedroom door in my face. "Fuck." I growl at the empty space as irritation claws its way along my skin. A moment later I hear the pipes in her ensuite coming to life. Fuck Evie, if she wants a reason to be pissed off at me, I'm going to give her one.

I walk over to the kitchen and turn on the hot water tap. A second later I hear Evie screeching, and I can't help but smile. I turn the water off and wait a full minute before doing it again. Her scream is shrill, and I smirk as a savage satisfaction consumes me. I keep playing with the water every few minutes till the pipes die down. I busy myself setting up the sawhorse and some of my tools, when Evie comes crashing out of her bedroom. Her wet hair is frizzy and untamed, her skin flush and her face twisted in an angry hate mask as she scowls.

"That wasn't funny!"

"I have no idea what you're talking about." And yet even as I speak, a smirk slides its way uncontrollably across my face.

She stomps to the kitchen where her handbag is thrown haphazardly on the counter, rips it off and shoves her hand through before turning to give me one last look. "You want me gone? Fine! I'm gone."

She marches out of the house without a backwards

glance and stomps away down the road looking annoyed and flustered.

Fucking perfect.

EVIE

I check the clock for the hundredth time and push away another empty cup. I've been sitting here for hours. Watching the tourists and locals laugh and talk and enjoy each other's company while I sit in exile waiting for my anger to die down. Anger is such an easy emotion; it hides everything else and it's easy to grab onto, and I do, because if I don't, all these other emotions it masks might come bursting to the surface, and I'm tired of letting them control me. I'm tired of shedding tears for someone who doesn't deserve them.

I get up even more annoyed and make my way back to the house. The town is sprawling with tourists and feels too busy, too full. In a place that's teeming with couples, holiday makers and locals enjoying the summer sun, I just want to be alone.

I stop in front of the house. His truck still sits in the driveway, the load of wood that weighed it down in the morning now offloaded and the whirring of a circular saw leaks from inside.

I draw in breath, seeking to steel my frayed nerves, and walk through the door.

The salty breeze tickles my face and the sounds of the saw die away as I step further inside. The furniture is covered in sheets of plastic which in turn are layered in fine white dust. Like light snow has fallen in the house. A few power tools line the walls, and timber beams are piled up in a neat stack.

I freeze for a second as I catch movement, and Liam walks into the foyer. His clothes are covered in the same fine dust, and he stops. We eye each other for an uncomfortable moment.

"Are you almost done?"

"No." He looks behind him where the gaping hole in the roof hangs open like a hungry mouth like it should be obvious.

I study his face, the harsh line of his jaw, the dark eyes, the hair peeking from beneath the cap. "I got tired of waiting," I hiss out. He winces at my comment, and I sidestep him, heading towards the kitchen.

"I'd like to take advantage of daylight. The more I can get through, the quicker I can get this done and out of your hair."

An image of his hand running through my hair flickers in my mind, and I beat it away. "Don't you need to get home to your daughter?"

His eyes darken for a second, and the muscles twitch around his jaw before he looks at his watch. "No, she goes home with a friend."

I purse my lips and feel the tension close in around us. His daughter; one of so many unanswered questions. My mouth feels suddenly dry, and I reach for a glass. "Would you like some water?"

"Thanks," he says. A ghost of a smile touches his face, and for a second I get a glimpse of the boy I used to know. Liam takes a step closer to the kitchen island that separates us like a big endless sea, each of us safe inside our own boundaries.

I pass him the glass, and his fingers brush over mine as he grips it. The sensation sends a shiver along my body, a familiarity that has me remembering things I should not be remembering. I jerk back like I've touched a hot flame and take a long sip, my mouth suddenly parched.

"How long have you been living here? Why didn't you find me? What happened to you?" I suddenly snap at him without thinking.

The muscles of his shoulders bunch up and his neck cords as he puts the water glass down. "Shit happened. Why the hell are you even here? You never come down here." His harsh tone startles me, and I almost take a step back.

"How the hell would you know what I do? And that's not an answer."

"Well, you haven't answered mine either." His deep voice washes over me as his lips thin and he cocks his head to the side.

"I think you should leave." I set my glass aside and glare at his beautiful angry eyes.

He tips his head in resignation, and his hands instinctively move to the belt around his hips as he loosens it. I can't help but stare at the corded strong arms and the tattoos that cover them. He catches me staring and gives me a knowing grin before he puts the belt away. "I need to pack up."

"It'll be fine. I promise not to touch any of your precious things."

He throws me an annoyed look and digs his keys from his pocket. "Whatever," he throws at me as he storms out. A minute later, his engine roars to life outside, and he drives off.

There's a long rumble in the distance as if the sky is

having a laugh at my expense. Fuck the sky, fuck Liam, and fuck this place. I throw out the remaining water from my glass and reach for the liquor cabinet, pulling out the vodka.

LIAM

The shower washed away the sawdust but none of my agitation. I've called Dylan back and agreed to meet him for a drink down at the Lion's Head. There are two bars in town, the new posh one with modern decor, too-loud pop music and a bunch of thirsty tourists. The locals visit it when they want to get their dicks wet for a night. The other one is the Lion's Head, an institution. One of the first buildings erected when they built this town and debatably still the most popular with anyone after an actual alcoholic beverage. With cheap drinks and a cheap atmosphere, it's easy to pass a night there, especially with many of the local men trying to pick up at the new place.

I tell Nessa that I'm heading out, and she barely looks up from her phone long enough to say goodbye. A part of me twinges with guilt, the part of me that feels that I should be doing better for my kid, be a better parent, spend more time. But as much as I love Nessa, she is a fourteen-year-old monster wearing the skin of a teenage girl, and she knows how to press each and every one of my buttons. Today I need a break, and she doesn't seem to care either way.

I walk into the pub and spot Dylan leaning against the

bar. He's chatting up his on-again, off-again, friend with benefits, Liv, and the way she is leaning into his words and biting her bottom lip, I'm guessing they are on again. I shake my head knowing it will only last a few weeks and I'll be forced to drink at the new joint for a few months till we're allowed back here. Fucking great.

Dylan spots me and winks at Liv before holding two fingers up and pushing away from the bar. He finds a booth and we colonise it before Liv shows up with two shots of tequila, two pints of beer, and a smile for Dylan that needs no explanation.

We grab our tequila shots and slam them back. The liquid is like fire running down my throat and ignites my belly. I slam the shot glass on the table and take a sip of my cold beer, letting it soothe the lick of fire left behind from the tequila.

"What happened to you last night?" Dylan asks between sips, his eyes tracking the shape of Liv's arse.

"Nothing, just needed a night in."

"With Olivia?" He winks at me, forming a circle with his thumb and finger with his right hand and sticks a finger from his left hand inside it. "Oh Liam, oh Liam," he cries in a high-pitched voice, earning us a few looks from around the room. I roll my eyes and punch him in the arm.

"Fuck off."

He laughs and takes another sip. "So you guys are getting serious then?"

"She keeps showing up uninvited, that's not a thing."

"You didn't complain when she sucked your dick in the toilets the other night."

I shrug. "Her choice. I told her I wasn't looking for anything serious."

"Speak of the devil..." His voice trails off as I turn around just in time for my eyes to collide with Olivia as she makes her way to our table.

"Fuck," I swear under my breath. I don't have time for this shit. All I wanted was a quiet drink with my one friend, talk some shit, maybe even laugh and go home with a fuzzy head before having to deal with Evie again tomorrow.

"Room for one more?" She sounds cheery as fuck as she ogles me.

"No."

"Sure," we say in unison, and Dylan shoots me a quick look. These small-town folks are all about pretence and manners; you don't turn people away, even if you want to, and you're always nice—but just to their faces.

I sigh and plaster on a fake smile, correcting myself. "Of course."

Her smile falters, but she stands by the booth waiting for me to slide over. When I don't, she lets out a little puff then bends down till she's practically sitting on me and slides slowly across my thighs, ensuring her arse glides along my groin before she shuffles off and tucks her body against mine.

Dylan's eyes glint with amusement. I grab my beer and take another sip. Maybe if I pretend she isn't here long enough, she'll get bored and go away. I know it's not fair, and it's not really her fault. Olivia is a great woman; she's intelligent and funny, and her tongue can do things that could make a grown man cry. A day ago, I wouldn't have minded. I might have even gotten a hard-on and taken her home with me, but today? Today I have only one woman on my mind, and I can't seem to pry her out of my system.

"Where were you last night? I called you," she coos, clinging to me, and my skin feels like it's crawling with insects. I notice Dylan biting his lower lip trying hard to hold his laughter inside.

"I just needed a night in." I tell her what I told Dylan, and she frowns a little.

"Trouble with Nessa?"

I know she is genuinely concerned about my kid growing up without a mother. She doesn't know who her mother is and she's never asked. There have been enough rumours about me and my family since I came back. I guess she has her own version of what she thinks happened. Still, I ignore her question and take another sip from my beer then turn to Dylan instead, asking him how things are going down at the gym.

He prattles on about hot chicks and hot yoga, and I let him, laughing at his lame jokes and crude sense of humour.

When I came back to Blue Haven, I kept away from everyone I knew. I had no interest in reigniting old friendships and looking up old acquaintances. In truth, I rarely had any growing up. The other parents didn't like their kids playing with the Morrison kid. My dad had a reputation that tainted Addi and I. We had each other, and I had Evie, till I didn't.

I ran into Dylan the first night I moved back here with Nessa. He was what you might call *loitering* in my dad's old place. I found him in Addi's old bedroom, balls-deep in some woman who was clearly faking it. I also nearly fucking murdered him, but the fact that Nessa was just outside the door forced me to keep my hands off him and at least get him to pull his fucking pants up, while the woman screamed like a banshee scrambling to cover up.

"Get the fuck out of my house." My breath leaves me hot and heavy as my fists tighten by my side. If Nessa wasn't outside this room I'd kill this fucker and throw his body into the ocean.

"Sorry, man, didn't know anyone still lived here. It's been empty for years." He's doing his belt up as he speaks.

"Get out," I barely manage through my clenched jaw, and the woman is already falling over herself to get away.

She walks past me then stops dead, looking at Nessa. She utters a surprised little 'oh' and gives her a startled smile. Nessa smiles back. "Hello," she says, and my eyes slice over to the woman who waves and says a subdued hi before making herself scarce. The man eyes us both before he leaves in her wake.

It's dark and late, and I check around the rest of the house hoping not to run into any more surprises. When I don't, I lock us up in my old room and we curl onto the old damp mattress. Nessa falls asleep in minutes, and I take comfort in her small body rising and falling, her sounds and her warmth as her small body snuggles into me. I hated growing up here, but I promise myself that Nessa will have a far better childhood than I did. The house is full of too many memories and too many echoes that chase away my sleep.

"**D**addy, wake up, there's a man at the door."

I roll over, groggy and tired till her words filter into my half-asleep brain and I shoot up, my heart smashing against my chest. No one knows we're here. I checked all the papers. How did they find us already?

"Stay here," I tell Nessa as my body bunches up and every impulse inside me tells me I need to run. The car is still packed, and we can be gone in seconds. No one would ever know we were here. I swallow the trepidation that tries to rip itself from me, fighting the twist of violence building in my stomach and head to the door.

I gulp the air that seems to choke me before my clammy hand wraps around the doorknob and I swing the door open, my body tense and jittery.

"Hey, man." The guy on the other side gives me a weird

uncomfortable smile and grabs the back of his neck as I try to work out what the hell he's doing back here again.

I suck in a long breath and stare at him.

"Hi?" he tries again and looks over his shoulder, shrugging. There's a car parked in the driveway; it's green and a woman sits in the front seat looking at us. "Leslie thought the little girl might be hungry."

"Leslie?" My mind is still trying to wrap itself around the idea that there are no cops surrounding the property, no one hand-cuffing me and dragging Nessa away.

"Yeah, you know, we were here last night." He smirks and winks, and pieces fall into place in quick succession.

"Yeah, right."

"Here." He shoves a plastic bag into my hand.

"Daddy?" Nessa's voice is too close, and I cut my eyes away from the man and to her. She's come out of the room even though she was told not to and is standing a few feet behind me. "What's that?"

"I told you to stay in the room," I grind out, but she ignores me.

"Hi." She smiles at the man. "Who are you?"

"Dylan," he says and gives her the kind of smile adults give kids whenever they give them any attention.

"I'm Vanessa, but everyone calls me Nessa." She beams at him.

"Nice to meet you, Nessa." He winks at her, and she giggles.

"What's in the bag?"

"I brought you breakfast."

"You did?" She's shrieking and runs up to me, snatching the bag from my hand and looking at its contents.

"Nessa." My voice is colder than I meant it to be, and she freezes. Her small face looks up at me, her eyes watering. She should know better than to accept things from strangers.

She pulls herself together and looks at Dylan. "Thank you."

She looks back at me as if asking if she's off the hook. Sighing, I tip my chin. She squeals and turns back to Dylan. "Are you going to join us?"

He looks as uncomfortable as I feel and shakes his head. "No thank you, Nessa, that's for you and your dad."

Her lips turn downwards a little as she endures yet another rejection. "Okay."

Dylan remains at the door, and I don't know how to end this situation that's growing more awkward by the minute.

"You've bought this place then?" he asks as he shifts his weight, and his eyes roam the faded weather-worn exterior nibbled on by the sun.

I don't want to get into it. It's not mine, it's my father's and he's been dead for years. Later today I'll head into town and find Michael—that guy has his finger in every pie and knows everyone around here. Maybe he'll be able to find me a lawyer.

"Needs a bit of love." Dylan runs his hand along the rotting doorframe, and I nod. Captain Obvious here doesn't know how to take a hint. "It's been deserted for a long time, so it's a good place to come and...." His eyes sweep over to where Nessa is intently listening. He clears his throat. "Anyway, might want to make sure your door stays locked."

"We'll be fine," I say, and his gaze swings back to me as if he's sizing me up.

"Sure." He gives a slight nod before turning away towards the car.

Thank fuck.

He's not two steps away before he turns back. "If you need a hand fixing the place, let me know. I own the gym on Main Street, come find me."

"Thanks," I say, step back inside and slam the door, not giving him any more chances to ask questions or offer any more help. Nessa and I have been alone long enough, we don't need help. I sigh; it's partial relief and partial frustration knowing I will now

"Another drink?" Dylan asks, sliding out of the booth and gawking at Liv. I have a feeling he will take a while with the next round. Normally I wouldn't mind, but tonight it means he's leaving me alone with Olivia who is already getting excited about having me all to herself. I'm going to have to let her down easy. Or maybe brutally. Either way, Evie is messing with my head, and until she's gone it's best I stay away from everyone.

Olivia's hand runs up my thigh, and she pushes her breasts against me letting me know exactly how she wants tonight to go. Her fingers trail slow tracks along my thigh, each time advancing slightly higher. Given that she has eyes, I'm sure she realises she is having zero effect on me. I let out a hot breath and am about to tell her I'm heading home when there's a commotion by the front door and Evie blusters in like a hot angry wind and crashes into one of the waitresses.

She looks stunned for only a second before apologising with a stupid grin on her face that develops into a chuckle. She offers to help, but the waitress waves her off, and Evie stumbles to the bar clutching onto it as if she's waiting for the Earth to open up underneath her and swallow her up.

I'm so consumed by watching her that I hardly notice Olivia's hand trying to sneak down the front of my pants. She mumbles something into my ear, her hot breath on my skin and her cold fingers brushing the edge of my boxers before I grip her wrist just as Evie turns around and spots us. Her eyes collide with mine before sweeping over Olivia and freezing for a long moment on her hand.

Evie's face transforms into stone, and she downs the shot she has in her hand before slamming the empty glass on the bar and stumbling over to the jukebox. I notice two things then; her denim shorts show off way too much of her long, toned legs, and every fucking male in the bar is focused on her and the way those shorts show off a hint of her arse. She presses a few buttons, and the jukebox comes to life. A second later the familiar intro chords of *Son of a Preacher Man* fill the bar, and the crowd howls as Evie starts to swing her hips to the music.

I'm mildly aware of Olivia saying something, but it sounds like background noise as Evie spins around and scalds me with a look before she starts dancing, or at least that's what I think she thinks she's doing as she flaps around trying to look sexy and failing miserably. Still, the sway of her hips and the way her hands run up along her body make my blood run hot and my cock come to life. I'm glued to my seat watching her make a spectacle out of herself, and I'm perfectly happy to let her be a fool until some arsehat stands up and thinks he can dance with her.

The second he puts his hands on her, I'm out of my seat and moving towards her. Who does this fucker think he is? She leans into him as he leers at her, grinding into her arse, sending a few winks around the room before he wraps his hands around her stomach. I'm on them in a few swift steps, and I grab her wrist, pulling her away from the man who looks pissed off and surprised.

"What the hell?" she screams as my vice grip tightens around her wrist.

"I'm taking you home."

"Let go!" she screams, and now every eye in the place is

on me. Like I give a fuck. I ignore everyone and start yanking her towards the door.

The man who seconds ago was dry-fucking her takes a step towards me. "The lady told you to let her go."

I spin around, squaring my shoulders and glowering at the arsehole, while Evie tries to wrench her wrist away. "I'm taking her home."

"Seems like she doesn't want to go home with you." He doesn't back down, his muscular arms tightening as he clenches his fist. I notice the black mamba tattoo on his arm. It feels vaguely familiar, but I shake away the thought as a few of the other men in the bar all shift in their seats, like they're ready to step in.

"Well, she sure as fuck isn't going home with you."

He shrugs all smug and sure of himself. "She's clearly not interested in you, so why don't we let the lady decide for herself?"

A few of the men are now standing up, and this is becoming a bigger spectacle than it should have been. Evie is not leaving with this guy full stop, that's a given. I hold in a delighted smile, keeping my face neutral. This guy has no idea who he's dealing with.

I release her, then turn to her. She's glowering at the both of us, her face twisted with fury. The dickhead does the dirty work for me, and I bite my lip to keep the smile from coming up.

"So, darling, which one of us are you going home with?" He actually winks, and I work hard at containing my laughter.

"I wouldn't go home with either of you if you were the last two men on Earth!" she spits out, and a howl of laughter picks up around the room. She spins around, her face stained a deep shade of red, and pushes her way out the door.

I vaguely hear my name being called as I follow her out, when a hand grips my arm. I spin around ready to throw a punch when I recognise Dylan. "What the hell, man? Olivia...."

My gaze darts over to the booth where Olivia is looking confused and pissed. I wish I gave more of a damn; she probably deserves better.

"Not now!" I hiss at Dylan as I shake away from his grip and walk out into the humid night. I search the street, but Evie is gone. She is quick for a drunk. I take off and find her stomping towards her house. Maybe her anger sobered her up. But even as the thought crosses my mind, she stumbles a little, and I quicken my pace. I just want to make sure she gets home safely.

I catch up to her just as she stumbles again. Reaching for her, I help her regain her balance. She turns to me in surprise, not expecting the touch, then pulls away, her face contorting in anger.

"Leave me alone!" She pushes my chest and sets off.

"What the fuck was that back there?"

"I was out for a drink and dance. You ruined both."

"Looks like you were out for much more than that," I shoot back, and she silences me with a murderous look.

"What I do is none of your business! You left, remember? You didn't want me then, and I don't need you now!" She's tripping over her words, and I don't know if it's the alcohol or the emotion.

"I'm just trying to help."

"I don't need help," she throws at me in a cold tone as she stumbles again, and I catch her, this time stopping us in the street, grabbing her hands and forcing her to look at me.

I don't know when she started crying, but two long streaks cleave her cheeks. She tries to shake away, but I don't let her. I hold her there, finding myself wanting to feel more of her soft skin, but not like this. "Evie, please."

She stops fighting and her eyes collide with mine. They glisten under the streetlight, her face brimming with a blend of emotions all simmering on the surface. She looks so fragile, but not fragile like a flower, fragile like a hand grenade about to go off. Evie needs to be handled with care, but before I have any time to think about my next words, to try and calm her, to explain...anything, her lips crash into mine in a brutal, deep bruising kiss. For a microsecond, I freeze, but as her tongue pushes into my mouth and my hands tighten around her waist pulling her closer, all my reason melts away. I should know better; I'm sober and responsible, but it's Evie, and my body will not respond to anything my brain is trying to say. Not when she moans into my mouth and her hands shoot to my hair, gripping the strands. Not when she arches her neck, deepening our kiss and pushing herself into me.

I can't help myself. I devour her like I've been starving since the last time I saw her. Like not a single minute has passed since the last time I kissed her. Like she's still mine. But somewhere inside me my brain jolts back into life pushing reason back to the surface.

I jerk away, breaking the kiss. "Evie." She stares at me for a few seconds, like she's been dazzled. There are a million things I want to say, to do with her, but she's not all there, and when—if—she ever takes me back, she needs to do it sober and wanting, and not drunk and desperate. "This isn't a good idea, you've had too much to drink."

Her hand shoots up, and she slaps me across the face before pushing away from me and taking off again.

I'm rooted in place, shellshocked. That kiss flayed me open, tearing at the old wounds I tried so hard to bury and slices open the old longing ache in my chest. I finally dislodge my legs from the ground and catch up with her again. We're not far from her house, and she's all but running now.

"Evie," I call after her, but she doesn't slow down. If anything, her strides get longer and angrier as she tries to put more distance between us. "Evie, wait," I try again when I'm close enough to touch her, grab her hand, kiss her again.

"Go away, Liam. I don't need a chaperone." Her scathing tone slices through me.

"I just want to make sure you get home safely." I'm walking a step behind her, everything inside me screaming for me to reach for her hand, lace my fingers through hers, just like pieces of a puzzle that belong together, and take her home.

"I'm home, you can go now."

When I look up, I realise that we are outside her house. I follow her up the driveway and up the porch stairs, watching her fumble with her key. She drops it, and I snatch it away from her before she can pick it up again.

"Give it back!" Her narrow eyes burn with anger, and my frustration with her stubbornness has my skin burning, or maybe it's because her lips were on mine not five minutes ago. I push away the thought and shove her lightly out of the way, slipping the key into the keyhole and opening the door for her. She gives me an annoyed look before stepping inside and putting her hand out for the key. I brush past her, walk inside and place the key on the little table by the door.

She lets out a small huff and remains by the door, slouching on the frame. "You can go now, I'm fine." She sounds defeated and tired, and her words are slurred and garbled.

I ignore her and take her by the hand, which tenses under my touch. It hangs loosely in my grip. She doesn't protest this time, just follows me through the dim house towards her bedroom in a pregnant silence that struggles to keep everything contained.

The bedroom is dark, only shards of light filter in through the open door. She pulls her hand free of mine and makes her way to the bed, a rectangular shadow in the middle of the room. She collapses onto the mattress, not bothering to climb under the blanket.

"Evie..." I try, not sure what to say, or if anything I do say will be remembered in the morning.

"Just go." Her stony tone is devoid of any emotion and chips at my heart. I nod and step out of the room, leaving the door open a fraction.

I stare at it, unsure what to do. A part of me, a huge primitive part that is yet to evolve, wants to rip that door off its hinges and go back inside, finish that kiss and take everything that belongs to me. But another side, the stupid rational side, the adult in me screams a reminder that I have a kid at home who's probably starting to wonder why I'm not back.

I let out a frustrated growl as I stomp out of Evie's house and back to the bar where I get into my truck and drive home like a madman.

I wake up to the sounds of insistent pounding and take a minute to realise the noise isn't coming from the inside of my skull. My head hurts, my mouth is dry, and I roll my tongue over my chapped lips. I groan and roll over onto my back, wishing for the pounding to stop. It doesn't. I roll over and grab the blanket, throwing it over my head. It's too humid and it sticks to my already clammy body. It also doesn't drown out the noise.

I blindly search for my phone. There's a faint beam of light coming from the crack in the door. Letting my fingers find their way in the dim room. I find my phone on the bed stand. I don't remember putting it there, and as the thought hits me, memories from last night start playing out in my head like someone has put on an old black and white movie reel, and I cringe, burying my head under the blanket.

I wasn't planning on going out. I wasn't planning on getting totally shit faced either, but I ran out of vodka and, somehow, by the time I reached the bottom of the bottle, my mind was still churning, asking the same old questions that have plagued me for so long. Or at least I think it was, because I clearly wasn't thinking straight when I left the house to go to the bar, and I sure as hell wasn't compos mentis when I started dancing. I cringe again, bringing my hands to my face and squeezing my eyes tight as if hiding could erase the embarrassment and stupidity.

I draw in a long breath as the rest of the night plays out in my head. So what if I kissed him? The memory of his lips against mine set my stomach into a slow roll, and my heart skitters at the way his hands gripped my waist and pulled me closer; how we fit together like two missing pieces.

But then those feelings melt away when the rest of the memory spills inside me like tasteless cold tea that's been sitting too long. He rejected me. Again. I clench my jaw tight, wishing it all away.

The pounding becomes unbearable, and the aching in my skull ebbs and flows like a cold tide. I need to sleep it off. Liam needs to go. I check the time on my phone, squinting against the too-bright light. I blink a few times till my eyes focus. 7.10 a.m. Way too early to get out of bed. But I'm parched, and that stupid knocking still hasn't stopped.

I drag myself to the ensuite where I find a glass, fill it with water and gulp it down like I've just escaped a desert. I fill it up a second time and down that one also. A few streaks of water escape and roll down my chin and throat, staining the front of my shirt. The glass thuds as it hits the porcelain sink. I splash water on my face, watching it drain away in rivulets that join at my chin to form a furious waterfall that splashes into the sink. Groaning, I pat my face dry and stare at the semi-open door and the noise seeping from beyond it. I know I have to face him eventually.

I'm still wearing the clothes from last night. I raise my hand to sniff under my armpits and my whole face contorts with disgust. Sour sweat blended with alcohol and leftover deodorant overwhelms my senses. A shower would take it all away. It would also make me feel insurmountably better, but the last time I showered with Liam here he was being a dick, and I have no time for his shit today, or ever.

I shove the heel of my palms to my eyes and squeeze tightly till all I can see are black and white patterns and spots that swirl in my head. I blink a few times before blowing out a long breath and make my way to the door. I am a raging bull, a ball of furious anger, a bothered bee and all my rage is about to be thrown at Liam in a burst. Except that when I swing the door open, I do not expect what awaits me on the other side.

His naked back glares at me as he puts down a hammer and stretches over to pick up a piece of timber. All the muscles flex with motion, and I'm fucking mesmerised. I don't know why he feels the need to work with his shirt off or why I can't help but look at the boxers peeking out above the waistline of his worn jeans. His body is strong and toned, forged by hard work. His corded bare arms show off his intricate tattoos and the stories they tell.

My eyes jerk away from his arm when he clears his throat, and my face burns when I realise he's caught me gawking. "Morning, sunshine." He winks at me, and I scowl.

"Where are your clothes?"

"It's hot." It is hot, too hot, and it might have nothing to do with the intense humidity building up outside. He shrugs and starts hammering at the piece of wood clutched in his hand. The pounding smashes right inside my skull, and I have to close my eyes for a second.

"You can't be here this early."

"I can." He keeps ignoring me.

"There are noise regulations."

"We're not in the city, princess."

"Don't call me that!" I hate it when he calls me that, and he knows it. I grit my teeth, and he barely spares me a glance before he reaches over for another piece of timber. I hate my body right now; it's doing all the things it's not meant to do, and my mind—despite hurting—is trying to fall off the track and follow. "This is still a tourist town and people need to sleep on their holidays."

"Not my guests, not my problem." He starts hammering again, this time using unnecessary force, the sound ricocheting inside my skull as it bounces off the walls. When he's done, he grabs yet another piece of timber as if I'm totally invisible. When he goes to place it, I reach for it and try to pry it from him, but his grip is too strong and I wasn't expecting so much resistance so that when he pulls back, the force propels me forward, and I stumble a little before stabilising myself and pulling back a second time.

"Let it go, Evie."

"No! You need to get out."

He pulls the timber again, me with it. "Let it go, Evie, and let me get my work done."

"Come back later."

"Later will be too late." The way he says it has me swallowing down a surge of unexpected emotions, like he's somehow talking about much more than this job and this house. "There's a storm coming. I need to finish as much as I can before it gets here."

I yank the timber from his hand. He's loosened his grip and isn't expecting it, and I stumble backwards with the force and weight of it before I let it clatter and crash to the ground at my feet.

"For fuck's sake, Evie, stop this shit and let me work." The muscles of his jaw flex as he sets down his hammer, climbs off the ladder and goes to retrieve the plank. I take the opportunity to sidestep him, reach for his hammer and run towards the door, where I release the tool and watch it fly across the front yard.

I hear the heavy pounding of feet that follow me to the

door, and a second later I'm weightless, spinning around before my back smashes into the wall, pushing the air out of my lungs.

"Evie." His choppy breath heats my cheek, and his eyes are fire, anguish and despair. "This has to stop."

I shake my head, gritting my teeth, too aware of the way his hands dig into the flesh of my arms pinned over my head. Too aware that with every breath my chest arcs just a few more inches into his. Too aware of how his waist pins me against the wall and how we're both totally aware of his cock hardening between us, pushing against my stomach.

"Evie." His forehead drops to mine, and I freeze in his arms, the small act feeling so familiar, so intimate, so *us*. But there is no us; there hasn't been in so many years, and all these feelings trying to play out inside of me should be dead and buried. But his breath is warm on my face, and Liam is no longer the boy I remember, but a man who has my body wishing for memories. "Can we just talk?"

"Talk about what, Liam? About how you left? Or how you had a kid with someone else? Or how you've been here for who knows how long and never came to find me? Why do you want to keep talking about all the ways you hurt me?" My words are harsh and angry, tainted with the pain that lurks behind them.

He winces at my words and his grip loosens just enough for me to get my hands out and push at his strong chest, but his body still pins me down. "Why did you even come here?" His voice is strained, like he struggles to believe I'm here.

It should be an easy question to answer, but it's not. I decide to go with the simple answer, even if it's not the whole one. "My mum made me."

His lips twitch in a sad smile that tugs at my heart. I'm not sure what he was hoping to hear. "How long will you stay?"

"I'll be out of here the minute you're done fixing the house. I need to get back to my life."

"Your life?"

"What's left of it." I shut my eyes, wondering what I have left now that Trent is in the ground and Liam is alive and well.

"What's that supposed to mean?"

"Don't worry about it." I shrug it off, but his hand clamps around my chin, forcing my head up and eyes towards his.

"What's that supposed to mean?" he asks again, slowly, forcefully, his eyes burning with intensity as he searches for answers.

"If you'd have stuck around, you'd know," I throw at him, wanting to hurt him, but then the truth spills out of me. "Then again, maybe if you'd stuck around, it would all have been different."

His face twists with sadness in an instant, and if I wasn't already all torn up inside, I might have felt his pain. In another life, I would have reached out to him, taken him in my arms, and we would have let that pain wash over us till it ebbed away. Now it was just a tsunami that drowned us both in its wake.

"I didn't want any of this," he whispers against me.

I push at his chest, and he takes a step back. My head falls back against the wall, and all I can do is shake it as I look at his beautiful face and lament the life we never had. "I can't stay here if you're here, Liam. I don't think you'll ever know how much you hurt me, how long I carried you and that pain. The truth is, it didn't kill me, though sometimes I wished it would have. It didn't make me stronger." Tears prick my eyes and I can't stop them falling, and I hate that they do. I hate that I still have tears for Liam Morrison. "The truth is, all you left is devastation, and I'm not sure I can survive you a second time."

I choke on the thick stew of emotion that bubbles inside my throat; anger, pain, despair, they strangle me, and a pathetic broken sound escapes my lips. "My head hurts."

"Well, you did put on quite the show last night." He smirks, and the tension melts away from his face. I roll my eyes and hide my face that heats up.

"Whatever, can you just go? I want to shower and feel human again."

"Is that an invitation?" He winks.

"Yes, for you to leave." I make to step away from the wall, but he's on me again, his arms caging me in place, his strong body reminding me of all the things I've missed for so long. "Move." There is no conviction in my voice.

"Evie, can we try and be friends?"

I let my eyes fall shut for a few heartbeats and release a long breath. "That's not a good idea. Just finish the job so we can both move on."

He lets out a long frustrated sigh. "Fine." His hand hits the wall above my head, and he pulls away, returning to his pile of timber and tools.

I stare at his naked back for a few more seconds. He's clearly not going to leave, and no matter what I do I'm stuck with him till this job is done. Retreating back to my room, I come up with an idea to get us both out of this.

LIAM

The door to her room clicks shut, and I wince, wishing I'd just kept my mouth shut. All these years later and she's still hurting, and like an idiot, I've just gone and tore open her wound then poured salt all over it. The thing she doesn't realise is that all that pain is just as raw and just as deep for me too.

I look up through the hole in the roof. The heavy grey clouds push each other across the sky, choking it like smoke. I do a quick mental calculation of everything I need to get done before it starts bucketing down, then swear, knowing I won't.

I'm still working on the bracing when her door opens again and the fruity smell of shampoo follows her out of the room. Her wet hair is slicked back and held up in a bun. She's wearing a white singlet that sticks to her body and short denims that show off her long legs. She's definitely filled out more since I last saw her. She used to be skinnier, long spidery limbs and straight lines; now she's curvier, everything about her is soft—and fucking sexy. I silently swear at my hardening cock and rip my eyes away from her, concentrating solely on the nail I need to pound into the wood in front of me. Turns out it doesn't matter what Evie looks like, I want her—even after all these years.

"Okay, what do I do?"

I turn back to see her standing at the bottom of the ladder, her hands crossed over her chest. "Huh?"

"You said the quicker you finish, the quicker we both get back to our lives. I figured if I help you, you'll be done quicker."

I bite my lower lip, but the smile still escapes. At least I manage to cover my laughter up with a cough.

"What?"

I forgot how cute she looked angry, her brows pulled together. Her mouth quirks and her hands rope around herself tighter like she's holding a demon inside her chest. "You? Work with tools? Last time I saw you try—"

"Was a long time ago," she cuts me off, and all the humour drains from my face. "A lot has changed since then."

I nod. "Fine." I shrug and point to a long piece of timber. "Pass that over?"

She eyes the long piece and sucks in a breath. Her head cocks a little as if she's psyching herself up before reaching over and grabbing the wood. It's not heavy, so watching her overthink it is entertaining and nostalgic.

She passes it over, and I cover up my smirk. She's always been one to overanalyse everything; every story, every book, every situation. It's part of her charm but can sometimes make you feel like you're constantly under interrogation. She never stops asking questions. The surface is never enough for her; she keeps scratching and scratching till she feels like she's found the bone, and even then she'll bite down and won't let go till she's completely satisfied. She calls it curiosity. I'm pretty sure she would have made a brilliant interrogator. Anyone would break under her relentless-ness. My smile spreads, but it's bittersweet. I know how much me disappearing would have gnawed at her. Having that empty well to fill with the need to know would have driven her more than just a little insane.

"What?" She scowls up at me.

"Nothing, just watching you overthink things as always."

"I don't overthink, I consider every eventuality and possibility."

"So, overthink." I'll never know why she needs to dwell on every single detail, why it's important to her if the sun was shining and what I was wearing and how everything made me feel. It's like she draws pictures in her head and needs every colour to complete it, but really, even if she will never admit it out loud, it the easiest way for her to show she really cares, takes an interest. It's when she stops asking questions that people need to worry.

"Whatever, I just like to know things."

"I know." Our eyes lock for a short instant as we both feel the weight of my simple statement. I shrug it off, put the piece of timber in its place and start hammering before she remembers she wants to know things about me and the past. It's not the best diversion, but it works, for now.

We work in silence for a while. She passes me timber, and I hammer it in place, saving me precious minutes as the sky darkens and thunder mocks me from above.

"How long have you been doing this?" she asks as she passes me another bracket.

"Since we've been back." Her face drops a little, and I wince. Fuck, I should have rephrased that better. I try to overcompensate. "So about seven years now." Her lips twitch downwards, and I know I've made it worse. "I fixed my dad's house after we moved in."

"Your dad let you fix his house?"

"He died."

"Oh...sorry."

I scoff. "No you're not, and neither was I when I found out."

"You weren't here?"

I shake my head.

"What about Addison?"

I flinch at the mention of her name. "She wasn't here when it happened, and she didn't know either." A very skewed version of the truth, then again, the dead don't know much.

"So where is she now?"

"Not in town." She's not. At least it's a partial truth I'm okay with sharing.

"Right..." She turns away, her tone clipped and irritated.

She goes quiet again. With Evie that's not always a good sign and could go one of three ways, but the way she's looking now, she's probably spiralling, reaching inside herself and making up stories, catastrophising a version of the truth without all the information. Filling in her own gaps. I do what I always did when I knew she needed a hand out of the whirlpool of her mind and divert.

"Tell me about your husband."

Her eyes shoot to mine. "Trent?"

"Was that his name?"

She tips her head. "Not much to tell." Her eyes fall away —she doesn't want to talk about him, but I'm curious. I want to know about the man she chose, about the person who replaced me.

"What was he like?"

She draws in a long breath, and her eyes catch mine. There's an intensity behind them that sparks something deep inside me. "Not like you."

"What does that mean?"

"He stuck around."

"Ouch." She doesn't react, and I guess I deserve her barbed wire and sharp tongue, although it's getting tiring. I climb off the ladder and face her. She's allowed her pain, but she can't shoulder it all on me. She made a choice. "You know I came back for you? Twice actually, but you'd already moved on. I get it, I left, but I never held that against you." I shrug as her brow frows at my words. "I was sure you'd come meet me that day. You out of everyone in this world would have come—I know how much you wanted your answers. But when you never showed, I knew it was over for you—*we* were over. I get you're angry, but you had a chance to come and get your answers, you just didn't take it."

"Never showed? What are you talking about?"

"The coffee shop?"

"What are you talking about?"

My mind wanders to that day, the final time I came back for Evie, the day I knew it was over.

It's a sixteen-hour drive, and my eyes burn and body sags as I pull up outside Evie's parents' house. I have no idea if she still lives here or where else to look, but she's the first person I want to see. The only one.

Nessa is sleeping soundly as I cut the engine and stare at the house. Last time I was here, things didn't pan out as they should have, but then, things were different. I was running, I was afraid, and I wasn't good enough. But now? I'm probably still not good enough, but I'm free to offer Evie the world, if she'll take me back.

I settle my chugging heart with a long breath and step out of the car, making my way up the stairs and to the front door where I knock a little more violently than I intended. My heart somersaults in my chest and my body tingles with anticipation.

Her mother opens the door. "Yes?" she says a second before recognition paints her face and makes her mouth fall slightly open. "You?"

"Hi, I'm looking for Evie."

Her face curdles as if she's tasted bad milk. "Evangeline doesn't live here anymore. She lives with her husband now."

She strikes the first lash, but I knew this was a possibility. "I'd just like to see her."

"I'm not sure the feeling is mutual." She grimaces. "When you left, you ruined my daughter."

Her words are like the end of a lashing whip slicing my flesh. "I had to leave."

"I see," she says as her eyes drift over to the car, and I see Nessa sitting up. She smiles and waves at me when she sees me looking, and my stomach drops.

"Look, I just want to talk to her."

"I don't think that's a good idea." She takes a step back towards the house, pushing the door closed. I grab it instinctively, and she scowls at me.

Fuck. I take a deep breath, calming myself, then drag both hands over my tired face. I need a shower and sleep and Evie. "Can you give her a message for me? Please?"

We look into each other's eyes, mine pleading, hers cold and unforgiving. She sighs as she breaks eye contact. "What is it then?"

"The coffee house at the end of Oak Street, tell her I will meet her there, tomorrow at midday."

She nods, almost resigned.

"You'll tell her?" I need to make sure.

"Tomorrow at noon. I'll tell her, but think very carefully if you really want to do this."

"What do you mean?"

"I mean that she has moved on. She has a good man with a future and prospects, she's smiling again and eating well, she's got a good career as a radiologist in the hospital and you showing up again—you'll confuse her. She deserves to have the life she's enjoying right now. What can you possibly offer her?" Her eyes travel back over the beat-up car that belongs in a junkyard and

not on the road, and where Nessa is staring at us with big wandering eyes.

"I just want to talk to her, I don't—"

"I know you don't, but you will." She sighs and it's weary and tired, and for the first time since I've known this woman, I feel like she might care about Evie so much more than she lets on.

"Just tell her."

She nods and grabs her door again indicating our conversation is over. I step back from the threshold and let the door close in my face.

<hr>

Pushing aside another empty cup I stare as another customer walks in. Still not Evie. I don't dare look at the clock, because if I do I'd know that I've overstayed by a few too many hours. That somewhere there is a little girl in a hotel room who's probably worried sick about me and, that despite the sky burning with golds and oranges, I can't bring myself to stand up. I can't choose to believe that Evie didn't come. I don't dare to dream that she has picked a life without me in it. I can't face the reality that she has moved on without me while I have been clinging to memories and dreams of something that never really existed. Our future.

The pit in my stomach grows deeper and darker as the waitress comes over and gives me yet another pitiful look. She doesn't say the words that hang on the tip of her tongue and pour out of every pore.

"Would you like another?" Her smile is half-hearted and more sad than happy, and I shake my head, asking for the cheque instead. She nods and leaves with my empty cup as all my hopes dissolve like salt in the rain.

"Liam?" She yanks me from my memories like a root

being pulled out of the ground, and the words begin to cascade from my mouth in a waterfall.

"I came to your house; it was the only place I knew to look for you, but you weren't around, your mum was." The lines on her forehead deepen as I keep talking. "I asked her to tell you to meet me. She told me you were married, but I didn't care, I needed to talk to you, and I wanted a chance to explain." She shakes her head as I talk and takes a step back like I've pushed her, but I keep talking because I need her to know.

"I was sure if I came back and told you everything you'd understand, you'd choose me. But when you never showed, I got the message loud and clear. I left so that you could have your shiny new life. I just wanted you to be happy." A hand shoots to her mouth, and as I keep talking, she staggers backwards again like my words are bullets hitting her body.

"After that, I didn't see the point of dragging along a dead horse. I had to cut off that rotting limb and carry on or it would have poisoned and killed me. I didn't want the memories of you to turn into something angry and ugly. I didn't want to end up blaming you for the things I did. So I tried to move on, like you. Tried to forget you. Because it was easier to pretend that I hated you—for moving on, for finding love, for choosing him over me. But really, all I really hated was every second of my life without you."

Her eyes glisten with unshed tears; they're round and large and full of disbelief, while I feel like the guy who just got caught with his dick in his hands taking a piss on a police car—helpless and stupid. "You came back?"

"Yes." I frown as my chest tightens.

"My mum knew?"

My heart rate spikes, and my muscles bunch up around my neck. "She didn't tell you?"

She shakes her head slowly, and red crawls onto her face as the anger takes shape, spreading like a living mask across her face. "She fucking knew? All along?"

She storms across the house, and I follow her to her bedroom, where she finds her phone on the nightstand. "I can't fucking believe her!" She reaches for her phone, and I grab her hand, halting her intention.

"It doesn't matter, it's water under the bridge." I try to calm her, knowing I'm probably going to fail.

"Of course it matters. *You came back!*" Her voice takes on a new pitch and anger blends with anguish.

My own selfish curiosity gnaws at me, and I tighten my grip on her arm. "If she told you, would you have come? Would it have made a difference?"

"Of course I would have come." Her eyes widen and her mouth opens and closes a few times like she can't believe I just asked that. My heart bangs against my rib cage with her words.

"Would you have chosen me?"

"Every time. You were it for me, Liam. There were no substitutes."

"And yet—"

"—No! I was broken! Trent put some of those pieces back together—or at least he held them together with gaffer tape long enough to make me enjoy his company and want to stick around for a while. At least with him, I have closure, I know exactly where he is."

"Evie, I'm right here..."

She snatches her hand out of my grip. "You moved on too." Her gaze darts away from my face, and I know what she's thinking. I'll have to tell her the truth... eventually.

"No, I didn't."

"There's evidence to the contrary."

I blow out a long breath as thunder grumbles above us

and lightning spears the sky with a serpent-like tongue slashing through my thoughts. "We need to secure the tarp. It's going to get wild."

"I need to call my mother."

"She can wait, this can't."

She throws me a glacial look that leaves no room for argument. Evie is a lot of things; kind, passionate and affectionate, but she is also stubborn, and once she gets an idea in her head it's almost impossible to change her mind. She swipes the screen and finds her mum's number. I retreat out of the room, taking my chances with the impending storm outside than the one brewing in here.

EVIE

iam closes the door and goes to secure the tarp. I should probably help him, but I don't give a shit about anything right now other than talking to my mother and finding out the truth.

"Hello, Evangeline, is everything all ri—"

"You knew he was alive?" I bark out at her.

"What are you talking about?"

"Liam, Liam Morrison, you knew he was alive?"

"That *boy*?"

Rage builds inside me like deep water currents, and I manage to keep that bundle of anger inside my chest. "His name is Liam. I need to know if he came to see you seven years ago, if he gave you a message."

"It was a long time ag—"

"Did he?" I hiss, feeling my control slipping away.

"It really doesn't matter now, does i—"

"Did. He?" My chilly tone cuts her off.

She doesn't answer, and waves of fury wash over me.

"Did he?" I scream into the phone, my patience worn through.

"Watch your tone with me, Evie," she has the

audacity to say, and I regret not being in the same room as her as I picture myself strangling her, slowly, till her eyes pop out of her skull and she's begging me to stop.

"Did he?" I repeat again, demanding an answer, ignoring her reprimand.

"Yes, he came over a few years back—"

Her answer sends me past my tipping point. I don't think I've ever felt so much raw burning rage that seeks to harm. "Why didn't you tell me?"

She sighs dramatically, and my whole body shakes, needing an outlet. The silence that follows stretches between us like a tight bow-string, and my anger ripples inside me. But before I have a chance to ask again, she starts speaking. "You were with Trent, you were happy, you were moving on."

"You had no right to make that call."

"I did what was best for you."

"You've never known what's best for me!"

"Evangeline—"

"Don't!" I lash out at her, my temper boiling over in a volcanic rage.

"You're being dramatic. It's in the past. None of it matters. You had Trent, you got to have all the things you ever wanted."

"You mean all the things *you* ever wanted."

"Maybe I should call Dr. Marshall."

"I don't need Dr. Marshall, and I don't need you trying to run my life!" I hang up before she says anything else. Thunder crackles across the sky, echoing my anger.

I barge out of the room and look for Liam. When I don't find him inside, I rush outside around the house and find him on the roof, where he's securing the tarp as best he can. His back strains under the heavy rocks and planks he sets over the thick blue plastic, which he'd already secured with his nail gun.

"Why didn't you try harder to find me? Why did you just give up?" I call up at him, waves of fury washing over me.

He looks over the edge of the roof, then climbs down the ladder before coming to stand in front of me.

"Evie—"

"You should have come back, tried harder! You let her ruin everything!"

"What did you want me to do? Chase ghosts? Come to your house every day and wait for you? You didn't show, I had a kid, we both made choices."

I scoff. "You and my mother made all my choices for me."

"Don't—" His phone rings, cutting off his words, and he brings it to his ear. "Yes, are you okay? I'll be right there." Turning back to me, he stuffs the phone back into his pocket. "I need to go."

"Go? But—"

"Sorry, Evie, look, can we finish this later?" He's already walking away from me.

"No! Stay here and talk to me."

"I can't, I have to go." His eyes dart between me and his truck.

"Well, seems like you've made your choice."

"Evie—"

"It's fine, I'm coming to realise I was never your first choice and never will be. You going and me not showing up is probably the best thing to have happened to us both!"

He doesn't say a thing, and his silence is harsher and colder than any words. He climbs into his truck, and a second later his wheels spin as he pulls violently out of the driveway and tears down the road and out of sight.

The howling wind picks up, roaring and groaning; bending tree trunks and pushing with it the malevolent dark clouds that shield the sun and turn day to night. I rush into the house and double-check all the windows and doors. The wind pounds against them, but it's the wavering tarp that whips about violently and claps inside the house in a menacing beat that worries me.

Outside the trees scream under the strain of the wind which brings the rain. It swoops down, in heavy harsh beads that crash onto the tarp. There's not much to do but sit and wait out the storm that feels so much like a mirror to my insides that want to rip and destroy everything in my path.

The downpour becomes heavier still, and an ominous creaking has me looking up at the large plastic sheet that covers the roof. It's sagging with the weight of the rain, and all I can do is watch and hope it holds.

I pace. I pace like an animal holed up inside its cage. My words haunt me, my anger follows me like a tyrannical shadow from room to room as I try to escape my own head, run from my feelings and hide from a truth I don't want to face. A sudden bright fork jabs out from above, zigzagging its way across the sky, followed seconds later by ear-piercing thunder that tears the silence into pieces. I scream into the empty room, my voice swallowed by the downpour, by the heavy sheets of rain that smash against every surface. The room briefly lights up with a flash as silver arthritic strings slice through the clouds with misshapen fingers, and another roll of thunder growls across the sky as a sickening sound like the crunch of breaking bones crashes above me, and the tarp gives way.

Water and rock and plastic and wood all explode onto the floor, shattering everything in their path. A warped tsunami of destruction that sweeps through the house soaking everything. I shield my face as water and splintered wood fly in every direction, and the house groans and moans in pain. Torrential rain pours in through the gaping hole left by the pregnant tarp. The wind lets itself in uninvited, pushing the heavy drops in every direction.

I grab the tarp and tug. It's heavy, waterlogged and weighed down by debris. It takes me a few minutes to push away the bricks and timber and pull it free. The wind picks it up like a sail, and it lifts, curling around me. I grapple with the rough plastic till I manage to tame it and fold it haphazardly beneath my arm.

I look at the dark sky and the relentless rain before another gust of wind slices through the house, and I know I need help.

"I didn't know who else to call," I say when Liam picks up, still sounding pissed off.

"What happened?"

My eyes sweep over the destruction of the house, where timber and rock and all his hard work lies in tatters. "The tarp came down."

"Are you okay?" Panic and urgency settle in his voice. "Are you hurt?"

"No, I'm fine, but the roof... there's water everywhere..."

"I'm on my way." The line cuts dead, and I stand in the middle of the ruined room with the tarp beneath my arm, looking up at the gaping hole that allows the teeming rain to wash freely inside.

Without thinking much more, I rush outside. The brutal wind is fierce, and the rain pelts my skin in vicious bites as I round the house. I find the discarded ladder and battle the wind, awkwardly gripping the ladder while trying to contain the plastic sheet tucked under my arm and wishing I'd taken the time to fold it properly.

Setting the ladder against the house, I cling onto the slippery aluminium and push myself up the rungs till I make it to the roof. I crawl around the precarious drop, slippery with water, till I reach the edge of the hole. I stare at the room below me. The walls drip with moisture, and the polished wooden floor is a swarming river that grows more swollen and deep with each passing second.

I begin to unfurl the tarp, but the wind catches it and I lose my balance. I fight the pull of gravity, and the plastic unfurls just a little more, letting the wind win. There is a second of weightlessness as I brace, and my hands instinctively close against the plastic as if it's something solid on which I can find purchase. My body tenses and waits for the sheer drop , when a strong arm catches me and Liam is there, his face set in a furious scowl. He's soaking wet, the wind whipping the rain onto his angry face, and his clothes and hair cling to him. He pulls me to him and sets me safely on the tiles, raking his eyes along my soaked face.

"What the hell were you thinking?" he screams as the wind tries to swallow his words.

He tears the tarp away from my grip and examines it before turning back to me. "I'll need you to help me," he shouts above the noise of the storm, and I nod. "Whatever you do, don't let go."

He moves to the edge of the roof and comes back with a nail gun, setting it down before he finds the hemmed edge of the tarp and indicates for me to hold it. I do as he says as he puts three nails into the plastic. He doesn't release the tarp all at once but in small, measured lengths. We work our way slowly around as the wind tries to push us off the roof and snatch the plastic from our grip. When we've covered the hole, he loosens the leftover plastic and nails it haphazardly into the wood in a strange, mangled ball.

He shouts something at me, but the wind steals his

words. He gets up carefully and starts to move again. I follow him till we reach the edge of the roof. He holds the ladder and indicates that I should get down first. I don't argue. I'm soaked to the bone, and despite the humidity and the heat, the cool rain has seeped under my skin, and the heat of the day has evaporated.

When we're both down safely, Liam grabs my wrist and we run back into the house, shutting the door and some of the noise behind us. I let out a long breath and look up at the tarp that stretches above the roof, flapping but holding. For now.

"Are you okay?" His voice is husky and low, and I turn to look at him. Rivulets of water run down his face and water drips off his clothes in streams.

I nod as he takes another step inside, and I take a backwards step, my heartbeat drumming in my ears as the rain smashes outside. "I'm fine," I say just as my teeth start to chatter and my skin blooms with goosebumps.

"Are you hurt?"

I shake my head. But he seems unconvinced. He grabs my hand and takes his time studying me like I'm a banquet about to be served to the queen and requires perfection. My breath hitches in my throat at his intensity.

"I said I'm fine." I snatch my hand away from him. He steps closer still, his eyes no longer wandering but locked on my face, then slowly raking along my body. His eyes blaze as he takes me in, my clothes clinging to me.

"What the hell were you thinking?"

"I was thinking that I needed to get that hole sealed."

"You should have waited till I got here!" His whole body seems to be shaking, but I don't know if it's the cold or his sudden rage.

"You were taking too long."

"You could have gotten hurt, Evie," he grinds out through a clenched jaw.

"But I wasn't so, no harm done. Thanks for your help." My eyes cruelly dart from him to the door.

"I could have lost you."

"You did that a long time ago."

He moves towards me again. "I don't believe that."

I scoff, trying to be brave. "That's your problem."

"You're lying, I know you still want me."

"I don't!" He's in my space, his towering body looming over mine.

"I'm sorry," he says and takes a step closer.

"It's too late."

"It's not too late, Evie. I love you, I always have. I'll never stop loving you."

I shove him away, but he doesn't move, instead, he takes a step closer and ghosts his lips over mine, sparking awareness throughout my body.

"No, if that were true you would have never left me."

He steps forward, his eyes boring into me, dark and intense. "I *had* to leave." He grabs my hips and yanks me to him. "I had no choice."

I push again, my stomach twists with indecision, fear, hate, love. I can't trust him but worse, I can't trust myself with him. "Everyone has a choice."

"And I'd choose you a hundred times over," he says before his mouth captures mine in a kiss that ignores logic or reason. With one hand on my waist and the other in my hair, he pulls me into him and sets me alight.

His body pushes me back till I hit the wall, and still our mouths battle, tongues gliding and dancing as my hands crawl along his shoulders and fly along his neck, into his hair, tugging him away, pulling him closer.

We are the storm, angry and raw, moving frantically, not

in exploration but in remembrance. My body screams for him as it recollects the feel of his, his scent, his heat, the way he makes everything inside me come alive.

He groans and the feral sound vibrates through me as his hands fall to my arse and he roughly tugs me closer. My legs instinctively shoot up and lock around him.

"You could have gotten yourself hurt," he says, and his anger ripples through his voice. His hot breath licks my drenched skin, burning it, setting my nerves on edge before his mouth finds mine again, kissing me with an urgency that defies logic.

He grips me tighter. I cling to his mouth, to his body, to his memory, and I breathe out his name, "Liam." I moan as his mouth leaves me and trails rough, hot kisses along my jaw and down my neck, nipping at my collarbone before his hand rips savagely at my shirt and takes with it my bra, leaving my breasts bare. He groans a second before his hot mouth closes over a nipple, and I arch for him, whispering his name to the world as my hands rove his neck and shoulders and claw at his scalp, through his wet hair tousled with the wind and rain, eliciting a feral groan from him. His teeth graze my nipple. Slowly stretching it as it plucks out of his mouth and he moves onto the other.

I whimper impatiently, grinding myself into him as he pushes me harder against the wall, his erection pressed against me. But then he pulls away, and my entire body wants to go with him, my mouth wants to follow his, and my hands want to stay wrapped around him forever.

He doesn't release me. He walks us towards the couch and lowers me into the soaked fabric. The world is a broken mangled mess around us, but I no longer care because each of his kisses glues it back into place.

He catches my wrists in his hand and places them above my head before his hands trails along the flesh of my arms, down my nipples, and along my stomach, eliciting a low hungry moan from me. His thumbs slide under my panties, and he yanks the wet fabric along with my shorts.

I squirm under his intense gaze, but his hands are back holding me in place while his mouth nips at my skin. My neck, my belly, my breasts; he's everywhere except where I really want him to be. He's hungry but patient, and mine is wearing thin as he decimates my sanity one kiss, one bite, one nip at a time. I whimper and fight his grip, wanting to feel him, to explore his body with the same desperate hunger I see in his eyes, wanting to learn this man I once knew, all his new edges and raw masculinity, but he scoffs at my efforts, punishing me with his tongue and his teeth and his hot lips that are simultaneously rough and soft.

"Liam." My voice is a demand, a plea, a broken thing only he can fix, and his dark eyes shoot to mine. All I see there is hunger, palpable and raw. My skin tingles as he releases my hands long enough to pull himself out of his jeans and boxers. His cock is hard and swollen, a bead of pre-cum wells on the plump tip, and my tongue instinctively rolls over my upper lip wanting to taste it. He catches the gesture and groans.

"Not today." It's a promise, and my breath accelerates with a sudden surge of future possibilities. The future; *our* future. The thoughts threaten to cloud my mind, but his voice cuts through the fog. "Stay with me, Evie. I want you here with me."

He lines up his cock and slams into me in one harsh movement, depleting my lungs and setting my body on fire. He stays there, buried deep inside me like we are the only two people that exist at that moment. His lips find mine, and this time the kiss is not a mess of frenzied desperation but slow and sweltering, worshipping, apologising, demanding.

When he pulls away, his fierce possessive gaze locks onto

mine as he begins to thrust, releasing a hoarse moan. Our breathing grows shallow as the slow pleasure builds inside me, gripping my body with bursts of sensation. My hips roll against his as my head tilts back and my back arches, wanting him deeper, harder.

With a finger to my chin, he redirects my face to his. His eyes remain glued to mine, finding the hunger that dwells inside, feeding on it. There is something in the way he looks at me; something old and familiar. A connection that cements our bond, the love we always shared, the one that could never be severed.

He drives deeper inside me. His deep grunts vibrating through me, his lips taste me, and his whiskers graze my skin. We moan and gasp, moving harder, faster. I rock against him, lost in the heated sensuality of his eyes, his desperate desires, as his hips pound against mine with delicious friction that has us both chasing the building pleasure, the desperate need for release, the intense desire to own each other. I grind against him as I explode around his cock, pleasure bursting inside me in shock waves. His mouth is on mine, swallowing my screams as his hips jerk erratically as we climax. And still, he kisses me as I pull him deeper, inhaling him, needing him, breaking for him.

His head falls to my shoulder as he heaves in lungfuls of air and leaves light kisses on my skin. "Fuck, Evie." His husky voice is strained and raw.

"I know," is all I need to say.

LIAM

I've let her sleep for a few hours, but I can't stand it anymore. I can't stop watching her, touching her, feeling her. She feels like home. Like the place I've always belonged. My lips skim her shoulder, and my fingers trace an invisible line down her smooth waist, over her hip. Curled up behind her, I'm moulded to her, and my body remembers how much it missed hers.

I kiss the spot below her ear, inhaling her scent, sweet and natural. She smells like a storm. "You're fucking amazing, Evie, you know that? I've fucking missed you," I whisper.

She rolls onto her back, and I sweep the hair out of her face.

"Liam." She's smiling, but the smile has left her eyes. She's deep in thought again and that's dangerous terrain. She doesn't trust me. Not yet, and I'll have to work hard to get her there again. I don't want to know what she's thinking because I'm afraid of what it might be, so instead of talking I kiss her, stealing the words away from her and drowning her in my desire. I want to strip her down to her skin and remind her just how intimate the bond between us used to be. I love her so goddamn much. I always have.

"Not yet." I seek her eyes. She sucks on her lower lip and gives me a slight nod. Jesus, that look in her eyes and the waves of her hair splayed around her, she's the kind of beautiful that brings a man to his knees. And that's precisely how I plan on worshipping her, on my fucking knees, my face buried between her thighs.

My hand grabs her waist and pins her to the mattress while the other grips the sheet that covers her, shielding her from me. I want to see her, really see Evie, revel in her. But I don't rip it away like I want to, fighting every base visceral part of me. Fuck, she twists me up inside, and I want to ravage her, claim her, but I contain my beast, allowing myself to linger in the moment, stretch it out, allow myself to believe that as long as Evie is still in my arms, she still belongs to me.

She gasps as I peel away the sheet, my touch on her chest achingly slow as the pads of my fingers reveal a hairbreadth of skin at a time. We watch each other as I pull the sheet slowly away from her till the hemmed edge meets her nipples and reveals her stunning breasts. I release a breath I didn't know I was holding as her skin flushes a delicious shade of pink, and my self-control wanes.

I continue with the slow reveal of her perfection, indulging in the hourglass shape of her waist, the contoured curves of her breasts, the smooth terrain of her stomach, her sweet, hot pussy. Her body squirms and quivers under my gaze as if that alone sets her alight, and it all unravels me. Her scent, her tempting silky skin, her little quivers of need, they banish all reason and everything else becomes a blur in the backdrop of her beauty. All that matters is touching her, kissing her, making her mine.

I fall to my knees at the edge of the bed and pull her to

me, spreading her open. The first taste of her is like a trip down memory lane. It's the first ice cream of summer and the first wave of the season. It's every blissful afternoon in the lazy sun and the first football game you ever won. It's every fucking sensational feeling packed into a single flavour—Evie. And I want to taste it forever.

My tongue punishes her in slow lazy laps that have her moaning and whimpering. They are beautiful little sounds that shoot right to my cock. Teasing Evie could become my new favourite hobby as my tongue circles around her clit. She moans in frustration, wanting to grind herself into my mouth, but I hold her down, controlling her, forcing her to endure my punishing pleasure. Evie is an edible delight. Her breaths become arrhythmic, and her hips fight my arms. Her nails claw at my scalp, pulling my hair, but it is only when she calls my name that I relent, the sound of it on her panting lips shooting a thrill of arousal through me as I release her hips. My hands make their way to her nipple, and I pinch hard. Her eyes widen for a split second before slamming shut. Her back arches, pushing her pussy into my mouth, and I devour her pleasure as she detonates around me. And I am undone.

I do not give her time to recover. I can no longer contain my need, nor do I want to. With Evie, I am raw and ready. I'm hers in a way I've never been with others. In a way I've never *wanted* to be with others. I crawl over her shuddering body and kiss away the last of her whimpers, swallowing her sounds and making them mine. I tower over her delicate body, revelling in the feel of her quivering chest against mine, her uneven breaths and the sweet fucking way her breath hitches as I push into her so easily like she was fucking built for me. All her walls clamp and squeeze me, and I groan as I barely hold myself together. My mind careens off the abyss, and I pound into her like a feral animal needing release. Her heat envelopes me and her nails dig into my back, my head rears back and my spine bows as my body tightens like stone, and I come so fucking hard I think I see stars. I pulse inside her, and she squeezes me tight. It's not just pleasure that I feel, but for the first time in fourteen years, I'm fucking content.

EVIE

Fingers of light pry their way through the closed curtains. There is a calm silence, and the smell of evaporating rain lingers in the air. Somewhere outside, birds chirp and kids shout, and I'm in my bed wrapped up in Liam's hot embrace. I indulge in the feel of his rough hands on my skin, the tickle of the sparse chest hair against my back, and the heat of his breath on my neck before I wiggle out from beneath him and find a shirt and some underwear.

I allow myself a slow minute to watch his beautiful face. The thing about guys like Liam is that you can't just love them, you get consumed by them, and when you do, you wonder if there was ever a time when you didn't think about them, or feel them, or see them in your dreams. I already feel that fire coming to burn me again, that obsessive inferno that has me needing him by my side, and I want to step away from it. Because I don't trust him, and that fire, that blazing unstoppable flame that burned between us, scorched everything and left nothing in its wake. Before it was thrilling, now, it's too dangerous.

I hate that I feel so much for him already, and that knot around my heart tries to loosen. I draw in a long breath and rip my eyes away from him, knowing as soon as I leave the room, I will shatter everything we shared last night. My heart pangs as I imagine what life with him could have looked like, thinking of the way he looked at me when he kissed me. You can't look at someone the way he looked at me—with the entirety of our past—without also imagining the future.

But we have no future.

I slink out of the room and confront the devastation of the living room. A pile of splintered wood and heavy bricks lie in the middle of the floor under the hole still covered by the secured tarp. The couch is waterlogged and dripping into the sludgy slow ravine that runs along the length of the floor and meanders around our discarded clothes. Shards of wood pierce the mud-stained wall, and unrecognisable knickknacks lay shattered and broken in tiny puddles littered with leaves and random debris.

I navigate my way around the disaster zone that resides happily in what used to be the lounge and make my way to the kitchen that has managed to remain somewhat unscathed. I make a coffee and step outside onto the deck. The garden is littered with evidence of the storm; amputated branches lie discarded across the green grass that seemed to have grown overnight, and a small creek rushes by the house carrying leaves and other debris. The air smells like earth and flowers, and the broken world is beautiful again.

I sip my coffee when the backdoor creaks open behind me. A second later his arms wrap around my waist and he kisses my neck, drawing me closer against him. "Why did you leave?"

"It looked like you needed to sleep."

"I hate waking up without you, Evie."

"You should be used to it by now." I wince at my own harsh words, and his grip loosens around me.

"I never got used to waking up without you." His voice is soft and strained as he speaks.

I remain silent, my throat clogged with heavy emotions.

"Last night was amazing."

I shake out of his grip and turn to face him. I've forgotten how sexy Liam looks in the mornings with his frazzled bed hair and his sweet smile. But now he wears a night's worth of whiskers, and his broad body is on display, and all the things he can do with that body smash into me all at once as heat pools between my legs. I squeeze my thighs, trying to concentrate on my coffee.

"It was." I finally swallow and find my words. "But it can't happen again."

"Why not? Me and you, Evie, we're inevitable."

"Maybe in a past life."

"Why do you keep fighting this? Us?"

I shut my eyes for a long minute and remember all the ways my body ached, all the ways my heart bled, all the empty years without him. "Because I am afraid," I finally admit and open my eyes to find his smouldering eyes looking into mine.

"We can take it slow."

"You have a kid, Liam."

"So what?"

How can I try to explain to him the way that makes me feel? That he loved someone else so much to give them this gift that walks around with his face and parts of him and another human being. That every time I see her, I am reminded that he didn't choose me, that he loved someone else more.

When I remain silent for too long, he takes a small step forward. "Come for dinner. I'll introduce you."

I shake my head. "I don't think that's a good idea."

"Nessa will love you."

His words cut through me like a dull blade. "I can't."

"Please, let me show you what I did with the place, plus this one is a total wreck."

"Liam…"

"Give me a chance to explain, let me tell you everything. Please?" He looks at his watch, and I realise it's the third time he's done it since he'd stepped outside.

"You need to go home and make sure she's okay."

He nods but doesn't move. His eyes imploring.

"Fine. Dinner." I relent under his gaze.

His face splits into a beautiful smile, and before I have any say over anything, he's erased the distance between us. His hands tangle in my hair and his mouth crashes into mine in a hungry possessive kiss.

"You remember how to get there?"

I nod, dazed, and his smile turns cocky. "See you at seven." He winks at me and runs back into the house.

I stare at the sky. A perfect sheet of shimmering blue. If it wasn't for the destruction that litters the garden and no doubt the streets of Blue Haven, there would be no evidence of the storm last night. In the same way that Liam is gone but my muscles ache and a few bruises have started to blush around my wrists and back. I bite down my smile and enjoy my coffee, letting myself indulge in memories of Liam's body. Wherever life has taken him, it's taught him more than just a few tricks about a woman's body and her needs. I shudder to wonder what else he knows, hating at the same time that he'd learned everything without me.

I blow out the thoughts with a long sigh and retreat to the kitchen, the coffee now finished. I put the cup down and search for my phone amidst the chaos. I find it under the couch, a square puddle attached to the case. I wipe it on my shirt. I have no missed calls. I'm not even a little surprised. I steel myself and call her.

"Evangeline. Why didn't you call?"

"I just did."

"Earlier?"

"I was busy."

"Doing what?"

Images of Liam's body moving over mine, his lips kissing my body, my skin heating in pain and pleasure as his teeth clamp down and drag slowly, all flash like slides inside my head. "I was sleeping. I had a late night."

"Have you started drinking again?"

I consider telling her that that was the night before, but I swallow down my sarcasm. "It was noisy."

"Is there much damage?"

I survey the scene around me, like a slasher movie for household items. I'm too tired to sugar coat it. "Yes."

"Well, make sure you take pictures of everything before you clean up so I can send them to the insurance company. Bloody incompetent builder."

"It's not his fault."

"Of course it is. If he did his work properly, I wouldn't be in this situation."

"You?" I blink a few times and shake my head as she keeps talking.

"Now I'll have to pay him twice for being incompetent."

I grind my teeth and grit out, "It was a category three hurricane."

"He should have been prepared. I'm tired of useless people. I should deduct the cost of the damages from his pay."

She blathers on for a while, blaming everyone but God for the state of the house. When she's done with her tirade, she reminds me to take photos of everything again. "And don't be lazy. Be meticulous, you know how these insurance companies can be."

I squeeze my eyes shut. "I'm fine by the way."

"Obviously. You called, late as usual—but nevertheless."

I bite the inside of my cheek and hold my anger at bay, just.

"I'll be waiting for those pictures. Please don't take all day about it, I have things to do."

The line goes dead, and I set my phone on the kitchen bench, picking up my empty coffee cup instead and throwing it across the room with a shriek. It smashes against the wall, leaving behind a tiny dent and a brown stain that leaks in a lazy river down to the ground. I'm in search of more things to break when a voice calls out from the front door.

"Hello?"

"Mr. Daily?" I call back to the voice as Michael's face comes poking around the corner.

"Morning, Evangeline, I thought you might need a hand." His eyes travel the length of my mother's nightmare, and I'm filled with gratitude.

"How—"

"Liam called, he said the tarp came off last night and you might need a hand to clean up."

At the sound of his name, my heart dislodges and bounces around my rib cage for a few crazy seconds, and I feel ridiculous, like a teenager in heat. I brush away the warm buzzing in my stomach and smile at Michael. "Yes, thanks."

"No problem. I have some things in the car."

He vanishes again, and I grab my phone, taking a few snappy pictures for my mother. Fuck her and her insurance claims.

When Michael is back, he has two buckets, some heavy-duty brooms, and a squeegee. I tie up my hair and grab a bucket, getting to work.

Michael runs his hand along the scratched coarse wall and sips his coffee, taking a final look around at our handy work. The shards of shattered wood and broken slats have been removed and dumped in the back of his truck along with branches, broken glass and other debris that poured into the house. The floor is dry again, albeit stained and dented in a few areas where the bricks smashed through the roof. The mud has been swept and washed away, and the house feels as if it has released a breath. The perfection my mother chased after, erased and dented; it almost feels lived in, normal.

"He did a fine job rebuilding this place. He'll do just as fine a job when he fixes it again."

"Liam did this?"

Michael's light blue eyes find mine, a gentle smile on his face as he nods. "You didn't know?"

I shake my head.

"Well, when he came back, he moved back into the old Morrison property. It was so rundown it wasn't safe for him and that girl of his. She was, of course, much younger then, and so inquisitive." His delight at the memory tips over to the rest of his face and his smile broadens, forcing an angry jealous wave to crash inside my body. "He was so lost back then, and when he learnt about his father, well, I don't know if it was relief or sadness. That whole history is muddied; an entire family vanishes without a trace and only the son returns with a story full of holes."

I frown at his words, but he carries on as if he didn't even notice he'd twisted from a light tone to something far more ominous in the space of a few words.

"When he came asking for help, I set him up with Florian; he was a few years from retirement anyway and that house was a great way to end his career. Taught Liam everything he knew, helped him get certified. Passed last year with a sudden coronary. Guess he couldn't let go of his love for beer and fried liver."

I have a thousand questions swirling in my mind, these tit bits of information are not enough to sate my curiosity and a scalding fire sparks beneath my skin, humming with heat and intensity. I set the questions aside, hoping most of them would be answered over dinner.

"He got certified fixing his dad's house?"

"Well, that and a few other projects around town. Turns out he had a knack for it. Once when Florian was really drunk, he told me the wood would speak to Liam in a way it never did to him. I put it down to the mutterings of an old drunk fool, but he was right, that boy is talented with his hands."

A shiver runs through me as I think about his very talented hands all over me the night before and feel heat singe my cheeks.

"And then he did the interior here?"

"Whatever your mother wanted, he accommodated for."

"Did she know?"

"Know what, dear?"

"About Liam building this house?"

His free hand turns up and his shoulders bunch together. "I don't know, she just approved the work and paid the bills. If she knew anything else, you'd have to ask her. Does it matter?"

Of course it matters. I shake my head.

"I must admit when he came back, I was surprised it

124

wasn't with you." He smiles again, almost nostalgic. "The two of you were inseparable as kids, and when he left to live with you, we all thought that was it for the two of you; a fairy tale ending."

I shrug. "I guess we were more like Romeo and Juliet than Cinderella and Prince Charming."

His mouth tips up in a little smile. "Well, seems to me your story hasn't quite come to its end yet."

I purse my lips together, feeling way too uncomfortable speaking about any of this to this man. As if reading my mind, he stands and places his empty cup on the kitchen bench. "Well, seems like we got most of the mess sorted." His eyes scan over the lounge which is now mostly bare and beaten. "Sure there are a few other folks out there who could use a hand today."

"Of course." I escort him to the front door where I lean over the doorframe and watch him walk towards his truck. "Thanks for your help, Mr. Daily."

He tips his head and gives me one of his signature smiles and a quick salute before climbing in and driving off.

I pull out my phone, looking at the time only to find six messages from my mother, demanding her pictures. I roll my eyes. It's almost four o'clock, and I have a dinner in three hours. My mother can wait.

LIAM

Headlights slice the path up to the house. My father was a useless piece of shit, but the two good things he managed to do in his unmemorable pathetic life was to keep our acreage untouched by the developers that kept sniffing at our doorstep, and leave me this property when he died. I've managed to keep it fairly isolated on this cliff top, keeping the tourists and noise away from Nessa and myself. And most importantly, I get to keep my own slice of paradise; a small piece of the ocean that's private and only ours.

I know I told Evie I would introduce her to Nessa, but we need time, and she's not ready. We have things to talk about, old scars to scratch. Tonight is going to be about us. I've sent Nessa off to Julie for the night, again. She only pretended to care for a few minutes before rushing to her room and packing a bag. Of course, I'd had to make some promises and grovel for forgiveness for vanishing in the middle of the night during a fucking hurricane, but she was safe and slept through it and wouldn't have known I was gone at all, till I walked in in my soaked clothes and gave her some lame excuse.

I'm jittery as I check on the roast in the oven and grab myself a beer. For fuck's sake, it's not the first meal I've shared with Evie. It's not the first anything I've shared with Evie, but I know what tonight means. It's not just a dinner, it will be an inquisition.

My heart dips in my chest when the inevitable knock on the door comes, and I settle myself with a long gulp of my beer before opening the door for her. She's standing there all smiles, and that nervous energy washes over me again—it's like seeing her for the first time after I realised I loved her.

I made plans to meet her by the ice cream shop. We were going to grab a cone and walk down to the beach, but I'd had a big fight with my dad that day; one of those that makes you want to punch holes through walls and kill everyone. One of those that makes you feel worthless and small, and you want to hurt someone just to feel bigger again, to feel significant. I didn't want to see her. I didn't want to see anyone. I never did when I was furious like that, and most of all, I didn't want to be touched. I hated being hugged when I was upset. I'd rather calm down and be alone, but I promised, and I couldn't leave Evie waiting on a street corner. So, I went anyway, waves of anger rolling off me. The minute she saw me, it was like she knew. She walked right up to me and threw her arms around me and this peace just swept over me and relaxed me almost instantly. I knew then that my body was telling my brain what I'd known for months, what I'd been denying for years. She was the one.

"Come in." I stand aside and take another sip of my beer, my throat suddenly parched as she gives me a crooked smile before walking inside. It's her nervous smile, and it makes me feel better about the nerves that keep creeping up inside me. Like I'm a fucking smitten teenager that has no control, but that's what Evie does to me; she disarms me, completely. I love watching her; she looks stunning in a tight singlet and short skirt and the way her face lights up when she smiles.

"Wow, this place looks amazing." Her gaze sweeps over the front room that's been opened up into an open plan. The living room, lounge, dining room and kitchen, all in their dedicated spaces surrounded by double-glazed, floor-to-ceiling windows that show off the amazing view from this cliff side.

I know what my place looks like. I designed and built it while that lazy fat fuck Florian sat and drank beer and told everyone he taught me the craft. The only thing I really learnt was how I never wanted to end up. Dylan helped a bit when he wasn't drinking or shagging some girl.

"Are you hungry?" I finally find some words even if they are lame.

"Starving."

"That's a shame, cos I only ordered one pizza."

She throws me a death glare then rolls her eyes. I can't help the smirk that creeps along my face.

"Fine, if pizza isn't good enough for you then dinner will be ready soon. Drink?"

"Sure."

I go to the kitchen and make her a drink, given the performance from the other night, I know that her preference for spirits hasn't changed.

She takes it from me with a smile, and I keep pottering around the kitchen while she looks around the place, noticing all the details other people always miss. I love that about her and know that a slew of questions will follow later about my choices, and I can't wait to tell her about those. The other things...not so much.

I should be watching the food, but my gaze keeps slipping to Evie. She breezes around the house as if she's always belonged here, and in many ways maybe she has. When I built this house, it was never just for Nessa and me. Parts of me threw so much of Evie into here. I know she can see it in the finer details. When we were discussing our own dream home, she told me all the things she wanted; maybe a part of me always hoped that one day this house would be ours.

But it's when she notices one of Nessa's jumpers tucked under a pillow on the couch that she freezes, and all the smiles fall away from her beautiful face. Before she has a chance to bring anything up, I call her over to the table and set out our dinner.

"Just us?" She looks around as if expecting Nessa to gallop down the stairs and join us any second.

"Nessa is spending the night at a friend's house."

She nods, and I can't get a reading on her expression. Disappointment? Relief?

We eat in relative quiet, our conversation staying safe. We stay inside the perimeters; her job, her studies, my work. We don't dare venture out beyond the lines we've drawn in the sand. Not till later.

When our plates are empty, a long silence falls across the room, like we both know the inevitable is coming, but neither one of us wants to be the one who pulls the rug from beneath the other's feet.

I offer her another drink, prolonging the inevitable, but she declines, which makes me even more worried. She wants to hear this sober, but I don't have to be. I grab another beer while she makes her way to the couch and sits. She's suddenly a goddess of infinite patience, and I'm the clumsy fuck who keeps fumbling with empty dishes and indecision.

"Come sit with me." She's not really asking when she taps the empty space next to her. My head falls back, and I stare at the ceiling letting out a long breath before I relent. I guess it's time.

I lean back into the couch, not daring to look at her. I know she has questions; I can see them dancing on the tip of her sweet silent tongue, but she's waiting for me. I don't know how to even start. As if reading my mind, she gives me direction, like she always does, pointing me in the right way. "Tell me why you didn't come home."

My head turns and our eyes collide, and I tell her.

But not everything.

I am at work when my phone rings. It's Addi. Addi never calls me. When I pick up, she sounds panicked and out of breath as she cries into the phone. She needs help and I assure my little sister that I'm on my way. I hang up and leave work right away. Addi isn't safe and time isn't something either of us can take for granted. So, I tell my boss I have an emergency and that I'll see him tomorrow, and in truth, I have every intention of doing just that.

I wait for the bus, having already realised I can't take my car. When it comes to a halt at the station and the doors hiss open, I hesitate, looking over my shoulder. An agitated woman with young kids hurries me along, and I step on. Walking to the end of the bus feels like crossing the river Styx. I plop into my seat and let my forehead rest on the cold window for a few seconds, closing my eyes and drawing in a long breath.

My eyes snap open, and I stare out of the window as the sky begins to darken with a sheet of grey clouds. I look at my reflection, imagining Evie staring back at me, her beautiful brown eyes searching my face, looking at me like I am something more, someone special. At that moment, I almost wish she didn't love me as much as she did. I've never understood why she picked me out of every other human on this planet when she could have had anyone. I could offer her so little, and yet she never wanted more than my company, my words, our jokes and late-night cuddles. She saw me, the person I used to be and the one I've become, but she also saw another version of me—the person I was still becoming... She believed in me, no matter what, and I never wanted to let her down. I bat the thoughts away of I concentrate on my more immediate problem.

I needed to use the time to plan and find a way to help Addi disappear without getting tracked down. I spend the entirety of the bus ride Googling and making notes, making phone calls, and organising everything I need before reaching the terminal. I probably should have called Evie then, and I wanted to, but I was sure that I'd have enough time to leave, get Addi to where I needed her to go and get back. I was going to tell her everything that night...except I never got there.

I get off the bus at the terminal at Angel Falls. It's not as busy as I hoped it would be, but we can still make it work. I call Addison, and she picks up mid-ring. "Hello?" Her panicked voice is strained and barely a whisper.

"Where are you?"

"In the bathrooms, like you told me to be."

"Are you okay?"

She sniffs. "I think so."

"Were you followed?"

"I don't think so."

"Good, did you bring what I asked you to?"

"Yes." Her voice cracks a little, and I hear the fear behind it.

"Stay put. I'll grab us tickets and we'll get out of town."

"Hurry."

I hang up and my hands clutch the phone. I bring up Evie's number and take two deep breaths before I stuff it back into my pocket. Tourists climb up and down busses, and the first of the school busses just pulled into the station. Soon this place will be crawling with kids in uniforms and even more bodies, and blending in will be easier. Looking around, I scan as many of the faces as I can and take a long walk around the building, looking over my shoulder for anyone who might try to follow. When I see no one, I circle back around to the ticket booth and buy two tickets to West Rockford. It's as far from here as I can afford to take us, and Addi will be looked after there.

All we need is to get away, and once everything is done, I can go back. I'll explain everything. Evie will understand. But I can't think about that now. I have to think about my baby sister.

I lean against the wall near the ladies' toilet and look around and over my cap. When I see no one watching I knock on the door. I wait a few heartbeats before pushing the door open and sliding inside. "Addi?"

The last stall door swings open, and Addi comes waddling out and right into my arms. I haven't seen her since I moved in with Evie almost a year and a half ago, and her smashed face tells me just how much I missed. Guilt eats at me, but I push it down. I haven't been here for her, but then again, neither has my useless alcoholic dad who spends his days on the fishing boats and his nights drinking and sleeping with whores. Sometime between my mother leaving and the collapse of his life, he'd forgotten he had kids, and we've fallen through the cracks. So it was left up to me to look after my sister.

She was fourteen when I left with Evie, practically an adult. She had a job at the ice cream parlour and was going to school. When I left, she was fine. She was one foot out the door just like I was, but she was also a stupid teenager with a stupid teenager heart and a boyfriend who was too old and rough for her, and today I am going to do what I should have done a long time ago; I'm getting her out.

I release my sister and look at her face. Bile and anger rises inside me. Her right eye is nearly swollen shut and she's sporting a long cut above her eyebrow. It looks as though she's tried to glue it closed herself. Her lower lip is sliced down the middle with a long black mark that almost looks like a piercing. Her neck is decorated with a line of four purple and yellow bruises. My body tenses, and I grind my teeth, wanting to kill the arsehole that did this.

Addi doesn't say anything as tears carve her cheeks.

"Do you have the bag?" She nods and pats her shoulder, where a large backpack hangs.

I gesture for her to hand it over and I slip it over my shoulder before taking the cap off my head and passing it over to her. I fix it on her head, hiding most of the mess on her face and bringing some of her hair over her shoulder to cover the rest of the damage. I shudder to think what the rest of her might look like.

I have a million questions for her, like how she could have been so stupid, and how could she have gotten involved with such an idiot and if she's okay, but I don't ask. I nod and lower the cap. Our bus leaves in ten minutes. "Let's go."

As we turn towards the door, it opens and in walks a man I haven't seen before but that has my sister gasping and his eyes narrowing when his face lands on her. His lips curl in an ugly smile as he eyes me. He's broader than me and a few inches taller, muscular, tattooed arms that tense and flex in his too large white singlet. A walking cliché. I was almost disappointed when his smile broadened, and he didn't sport the required golden tooth.

"Aiden." She gasps and takes a small step back.

So much for not being followed.

"Where the fuck do you think you're going? And who the hell is this?" He talks over my shoulder at Addison as if I'm not even there.

"I'm her brother, and Addi is no longer your concern." I take a small sidestep, shielding my sister.

He sighs dramatically, like he's watched one too gangster many movies, and I set the thought aside, wanting to laugh about it with Evie later.

"Look, buddy, this is what I suggest. You walk out of here nice and quiet, and you let me take your sister back home, where she belongs."

"She doesn't belong with you."

He scoffs. "You're right." He tries to sound callous, but there is an intensity to his tone. "She's a used-up bitch, but she ain't going anywhere, so I suggest you get out of the way before I make your face as pretty as hers."

Rage takes over my body. I lunge, using the element of surprise to my advantage, fury fuelling my fist, but he is quicker than me and ducks out of the way before landing his fist on my jaw. I wobble as pain explodes across my face and my neck strains to one side. I'm momentarily dazed, and I shake my head, trying to regain my bearings. When I spin back around, he has Addi, a hand clasped around her wrist, pulling her towards the door.

"Stop!" she screams.

His hand is heavy as it comes down on her face, and the slap of skin on skin bounces off all the dirty walls. "Shut up!" he orders as she sucks in a sharp breath, and her eyes glisten with tears.

I no longer think. The parts of my brain that connect logic to actions have vanished in a puff of angry flames and all that's left inside me is a hot, burning fire which propels me towards him in a flurry of movement. I use all my strength to pull him off and away from my sister, and I throw him violently into the stall. He loses his balance and starts gripping at the grimy walls, but the floor is wet with water and piss, and he slips. His head hits the porcelain with a loud thud and bounces onto the concrete floor where he lays unmoving. A trickle of blood flows from his nose, and a pool of blood begins to collect around his head.

"Aiden?" Addi calls as an eerie silence falls inside the small toilet block. "Shit shit shit shit shit. Aiden?" Her voice rises as panic sets in.

All I do is stare at the big man lying lifelessly on the floor.

"Fuck!" I push my hands through my hair, my heart racing in my chest like an Olympic sprinter.– Did I just kill a man?

"Is he dead? Did you kill him?"

"We need to get out of here."

"Liam, did you kill him?" I don't know. And sticking around to find out is a bad idea.

"Addi, now, let's go." I pull her by the arm just like Aiden did a second ago. She is pliant and unresisting as I push through the doors and out into the busy terminal that somehow feels too bright and too crowded. I lead my sister through the throngs of people. It now feels like there are too many of them, whereas before they would have provided us shelter from Aiden, now, they are a barrier that slows us down. We have to hurry, and I propel her towards the idling bus that's scheduled to leave in two minutes. We push our way forward, and all I feel is people's eyes on us. I don't look up, just at the bus, our final destination. We need to get out of here.

With just a few steps to go, the doors to the bus hiss closed, and I pull her, violently closing the distance to the bus where I pound on the doors. The bus driver gives me a long look, eyeing me, his eyes sweeping over Addison whose face is hidden beneath the cap.

He opens the door, and relief floods my veins. I let Addison get on first, following her, and wait for the doors to shut again behind us.

We collapse into our seats, and that's when I hear the screaming. People rush about, and suddenly there is a hive of activity as they gather around the toilets. My heart slams in my chest, and Addi grabs my hand, squeezing it tight.

Somewhere in the distance, I swear I hear sirens, and adrenaline courses through me, sweat erupts across my body, and every nerve in my body stands on edge.

The bus lurches and rolls slowly out of its parking spot. Outside there is a commotion; people shout and point and look around, Addison shrinks in her seat and her grip tightens around my own. With every slow movement of the bus, my heart chugs and squeezes in my chest.

Outside the crowd has grown near the toilet block and people are shouting. Some are holding phones out trying to take photos of whatever it is they think they see. I'm struggling to breathe as the bus stops again and a young woman looks up to the bus. Our eyes meet, and I swear she knows I've done it. The bus idles, and my skin feels like it's about to burst.

When we move again, we turn onto Main Street, and in a few minutes, we're out of town. I let go a long breath and wonder how long I'd been holding it. Fear skitters along my neck and panic burrows itself under my skin.

The further we get, the more the fear and panic settle next to me like another passenger. Addison whimpers and cries next to me in hushed muffled sounds, and all I can think about is Evie. If there was ever a chance of me getting back, I had just erased it. I just killed a man.

All the plans I made have been shot. Everything has to change. I take a few deep breaths and try to settle the rising fear inside me, clearing my mind, then turn to my sister.

She looks shell-shocked and broken, and I wish I could comfort her, but first, I have to look after her. After us.

"Addi." She looks up at me. Her glistening eyes flutter through her tears and her stricken face is twisted with emotion. "I need your phone."

"My phone?"

"Just give it to me."

She tips her head before digging into her pocket and pulling it out.

"We need to disappear."

"Disappear?"

"I need you to delete all your socials."

"Delete them? Off my phone?"

"No, Addi, I need you to delete the accounts."

"But—"

"No, no buts." I suck in a long breath, settling my rising voice that has a few heads turning to look at us. "Addi, look at me."

She does, and all I see is fear and confusion as I take her shaking hand.

"What happened back there, it was an accident, it was self-defence, and now that it's happened, we need to disappear."

"Disappear?" Her voice is shaking and tearing my heart in two. The farther away we get from Angel Falls, the farther away I get from Evie.

I take another long breath trying to find clarity and air in the stuffy bus. Someone is eating an egg sandwich, and it infuses with the stale air circulating through the old ventilation system. I can taste it on my tongue, and bile rises in my mouth.

"Yes, disappear, it means we need to start from scratch."

She shakes her head. "We can go to the cops, we can tell them it was an accident."

"We can't, we left the scene, we ran off..."

"We can tell them—"

"No." A few more heads turn towards us, and I squeeze my eyes shut before I continue in a hushed tone. "They won't believe us. Look at your face. If we turn ourselves in, we'll both go to jail."

She gasps and looks down. My knuckles brush her jaw and tuck under her chin, and I coax her face so that she looks into my eyes. I hate seeing her so scared, so helpless, and I hate myself for putting her in this situation. This was meant to be a temporary solution; get her to safety and get her on her feet, and now? Now I have a plan that has to evolve and be much more permanent.

"Addi, I'm sorry. I didn't mean for any of this to happen, but it has, and you are an accomplice. We need to disappear or—"

"What about Dad?"

"What about him? He won't even notice we're gone."

"Liam..."

"I'm so sorry, Addi…"

I let her sob, let her tears soak my shirt as I hold her shaking body uncomfortably. "Shhhh," I whisper into her hair and try to comfort her as best I can.

"Addi, Addi, I'm sorry, I need your phone."

She unlocks it for me, and I get to work, systematically deleting all her social media profiles then switching it off. Once I'm done, I set her phone aside and grab mine. I swipe open my profiles and can't help but find Evie. Her profile picture is one of us. Her hands slung across my shoulders and her face turned towards me. Her eyes shine, and the way she looks at me flays my chest and leaves my aching heart smashed to the floor. It was always my favourite picture of us.

I stare at her name and anguish eats at my resolve, my heart lurching in my weakened chest. If I call Evie now, she won't let me go. She'll demand to get dragged into the shit with me and she will do it wholeheartedly. But one day she will wake up and realise that this choice I have to make will overshadow every one of her dreams, and she will never forgive me for it. My mind drifts back to her mother's words at the hospital that day; she was right… She can do better.

My finger hovers over the delete button and I falter. I should be heading home now, heading to the only person who's always made me feel like I could be more, but instead I'm running to an unknown future, going in the opposite way to the one person who ever gave me direction.

I delete the app and move on to the rest of my socials before I switch it off and stuff both phones into my pocket. I'll get rid of them at the first opportunity I get.

The bus rolls on and the sun disappears behind the dark clouds, only the road and uncertainty before us. Addison falls asleep, and I look out the window as the sky opens up.

EVIE

I swallow, trying to digest all the information he's just hurled at me. There is too much to process. I feel like a PC with too many open tabs just trying to grasp the information before I get overloaded.

"Evie?" He looks concerned as I remain silent, my mind turning over in frantic circles. I have so many questions but no idea how to start. I need time, I need silence.

"What about Nessa?" He's just confessed to killing a man, and yet there is more he's not saying. He's still holding back, and I want to know. *Need* to know.

He shakes his head, and I don't know why he is keeping it from me. What could be worse than watching a man die and running away?

"I need to get out of here." I stand and look around, making sure I've left nothing behind, then make my way to the door.

"Wait, talk to me."

I shake my head. "I can't." I feel claustrophobic. I need to get out. I rush to the door and swing it open, but the fresh air eludes me when I step outside, it's heavy and muggy and the black sky is heavy with stars that pull on the black fabric. Everything is unbearably hot, and I'm sweltering in my own skin, like a fly trapped in a spiderweb, getting wound up tighter and tighter in its cocoon.

I'm desperate for relief, and I start to run, bypassing my car and the old barn, towards the well-worn steps that have been carved into the rock. I descend towards the small piece of beach. I need the ocean now. I need to breathe.

I throw my sandals away as soon as I reach the sand. It's still hot from the sun and it slithers between my toes as I run towards the water's edge. My mind is a dishevelled mess, and it needs clarity. I discard my shirt and skirt as I run, and I don't stop when I reach the water. I run into it. My stomach drops and my heart skitters at the cold, but the deeper I wade in, the better I can breathe. I dive in, letting the cold water permeate my angry skin, creating a barrier, a shield. Nothing can touch me out here.

I wade in till just beyond the waves. Till the water reaches my neck and is a calm lulling sensation instead of a violent one. I lie back and let the current take me.

The shouting starts off faint and distant, straining above the waves, then louder and louder, mixed with splashing. Desperate frantic splashing.

"Evie? Evie, where the hell are you?" His voice is near and frantic. "Evie?"

My eyes jolt open, and I flail, losing that fine balance between my body and the sea. I sink and swallow a mouthful of salt water, and the water around me changes, displaced by a heavier body. My legs stretch out, searching for the sandy bottom, but before they can get there, strong hands clinch my waist, hauling me upright. I choke on fresh air as he drags us through the water and towards the shore.

His furious eyes are blazing. "What the hell, Evie?" His hair is damp, and he's still got his clothes on; his black t-shirt and worn jeans, they cling to his body like the dead cling to life.

"I just went for a swim," I say as his fingers dig into my flesh, then seize as if realising for the first time he's not touching cloth but skin. His eyes fall onto my body, covered only in my bra and panties, and a second later he puts me down and takes a step backwards like I'm poison.

"It's too dark out here."

I stare at him under the dim glow of the moon. His chest is heaving and his eyes are wide, and I realise he's worried, or maybe scared, or maybe they are a singular feeling.

"I'm fine. I just needed to think for a minute."

"In the ocean? In the middle of the night?"

"Yes!" I shrug, cause fuck him, cause who the hell is he to lecture me about what I can and can't do, about where I can think or breathe or decompress?

"That was stupid and dangerous." He's talking to me like I'm a kid, like maybe how he would talk to his daughter.

"I'm not a kid, don't talk to me like one."

"Well, you're acting like one now." He's too stern and too serious and he's ruined my peace. I needed it, I needed to escape my own head for just a while, to forget about this lost time, about his confession and just let it sink into me.

"Well, you're acting like one now." I mimic his tone, and all I want to do is shut him up. Without thinking, my fingers dip into the water and fan out before I slap them across the water with force, watching the stream of water break across his face and torso.

He blinks a few times before his tongue slips out of his mouth and licks the droplets away. And for a second, I'm locked on that tongue on those lips and heat spreads under my skin as if someone has just thrown a Molotov cocktail and ignited my insides. But I have no time to dwell as he turns his body before twisting around. His muscular arm summons a tsunami that drenches me.

"Liam!" I shriek and push my wet hair from my face, tasting salt water. I push his chest with both arms, having no effect on him whatsoever. In retaliation, he grabs my waist, and my feet leave the sandy ground below. I claw at his arms and try to reach for the safety of his body. "Don't!" I beg. "Don't." But it's too late. My entire body sinks under, feet, waist, face. I'm a sinking anchor and he's let go of my chain.

I shoot up, searching for him, wanting to punish him for his devious deed. Chasing his dark silhouette and pushing him, he brushes me off and every other attempt I make at drowning him, till I have no choice but to latch onto him, locking my legs around his waist and grabbing his shoulders, pulling, tugging trying to drag him down with me.

But of course, he's too strong and he leans backwards instead, till I'm thrown against him. I'm giggling so hard. I don't know when we started laughing, it doesn't really matter because the laughter stops when our foreheads touch and his lips close around mine, and my tongue slips inside his mouth.

He stands there, shouldering my weight, and I peel his shirt away before capturing his mouth with mine once more and reaching down for the zip of his jeans. I tug against the waves and water that seem to want to keep them glued to his body.

I inhale his pained groan when I feel his hard cock between us, and he curses against my lips. Ripping at my underwear and bra, sending them away with the waves like lost letters in empty bottles.

He starts to move, manoeuvring through the waves and guiding us towards the shore. My body escapes the water inch by inch, and I should be shaking with cold, but it's anticipation, it's the want that has my body trembling.

We reach the shore, and we fall to the sand, not violently, but not softly, somewhere in the middle, just like how we've always been.

He thrusts inside me with one easy move, and I moan as my body is set alight. His hands find my hair, fisting the wet mess and he tugs, grunting and moving inside me like he might die if he stops. He's just like the ocean we just left; calm and violent all at once.

My nails bite into his skin as his mouth closes in on mine, and I never want him to stop. I never want to stop kissing him, inhaling him, drowning in him.

The truth is that Liam never stopped loving me, in the same way that I never stopped loving him, and here, in this moment, we can both taste that truth in our sweat and salt and raw hungry kisses—this is real—it's fucking real.

I can't catch my breath as pleasure builds inside me, a quivering, sandy, wet mess beneath his hot strong body. He's no longer the ocean, the calm waves of his movement now a stormy tempest as he pounds into me, relentless, angry, desperate, and I explode around him, screaming out his name into the dark night above us, wishing on every fucking star that stares down on us that it could be like this forever. But as he stiffens above me and jerks, growling out my name like it's both a blessing and a curse, I know it can't be.

For a moment, the whole world stills, and then his forehead is back on mine and his eyes shine like the stars above us as he grins down on me. "Fuck, Evie."

Fuck.

He rolls onto his back and sucks in long gulps of air. I look at his beautiful face; the face I have loved for so long. The man I hoped would make me laugh for a lifetime.

But he won't tell me the whole truth and our trust is so fragile and hesitant. He's given me what he is willing, and as long as he keeps the rest from me, I can never really trust him, never be sure he'd stay, never really know if I was his first choice.

He turns his head to me as the rising and falling of his chest slows down and he smiles, a smile so beautiful it almost shatters my resolve as it wrenches my heart.

He reaches for me, and I flinch away, then jump up and run. He's calling my name again, and I know he'll come chasing, but this time I can't allow myself to get caught, because this time I might not be strong enough to leave.

I scale the slippery stairs. The sand that minutes ago caressed me in a soft blanket now grains and exfoliates against my skin. His voice fades, and I chance a look back. His dark silhouette on the beach flails its arms as he hops, either pulling up his soaked jeans or tearing them off his ankle. I don't stick around to find out but make it back to the top of the cliff where I sprint back to the house. I find one of his discarded shirts, it lies limp on the banister, and I grab it, shucking it on before I find my keys and bolt for the door. I slam the door to my car just as he appears over the cliff. He's sprinting towards me, shouting my name, but I put the car into drive and race into the darkness.

***

I almost miss the car in the driveway as I slam on the brakes, coming to an abrupt stop inches from it. I grip my steering wheel, letting my head fall back and let out a singular sharp breath before I step out and make my way into the house.

She's in the lounge, taking in the cleaned-up space and remaining damage on the walls. Her phone snaps a picture.

Her head whips towards me as I walk in, and a scowl crawls on her face.

"What are you doing here?"

"It's my house, and you didn't answer your phone." Her eyes rake along my body, and I can't imagine what she might be thinking as I try to get past her, my body still peppered in sand, his shirt that smells of him draping off one shoulder, coming to midway down my thighs and covering my nudity.

"I was busy."

"I told you to send me pictures."

"I was busy," I say again. I have no patience for my mother, and her presence is like salt on an open raw wound.

She reaches for me, her face bends in distaste as she pushes a wet clump of hair from my face. "Evangeline, look at you, you're a mess."

"So what? So let me be a fucking mess."

"Language, Evie." She purses her lips, ignoring me. "We need to call Dr. Marshall. We need to fix you."

I laugh in her face, a demented bitter sound. "You can't fix this." I wave at myself. "You can't just throw money at a doctor and pills in my direction and hope to quash all my feelings again. I *want* to feel, I want to bleed, I want to ache, fuck it, I deserve to." I shake my head as anger boils inside me. "I've earned these feelings, these heartbreaks, the scars they will leave on my heart, and you're not going to steal them from me."

"Evie—"

"No! All you've ever done is resent me. All you've ever done is force me on a path you never got to walk down. I don't want your life! I don't want everything to be okay all the time. I want the anger and the mess. I want the sadness because it makes all those other feelings so much sweeter."

"Evangeline, you're delusional. I'm calling Dr. Marshall." She lifts the phone and swipes the screen. As always, my words wash over her, meaningless, invisible like I am. Reaching for it,

I grab it from her hand and throw it with all my strength at the wall. The screen shatters and a small piece of casing flies and skitters across the floor. "Evie! What has gotten into you?"

"You! You and your poisonous, insidious hatred of everything about me and every choice I make. Just leave me alone!"

"But I'm your mother, Evie, it's my job to—"

"Love me! That was your only job ever, and you could never do it," I hiss at her because my anger feels wasted. I storm out of the room and into the bedroom where I stuff my clothes into my bag. I tear off Liam's shirt, pretending it doesn't hurt to discard it, before slipping into my own clothes. They grind and pull against the sand still stubbornly holding on to parts of me like glitter that embeds itself into everything. But this sand will wash off and disappear down the drain along with all these new memories. Liam Morrison is a bad idea and thinking I could trust him again was a worse one.

I march past my mother who is standing in the lounge half shell-shocked half annoyed, ignoring her calls. I don't stop as I walk out the door to my car and leave this fucking place behind me.

I pull up to the house not recognising the car parked in the driveway and walk in expecting to find Evie. We need to finish out conversation. I hate that she ran away from me last night, given what we shared, but I tried to understand her needs, give her space, but today we have to talk, finish this game. Evie belongs to me, and I belong to her and denying it any more is like trying to pretend that the sun won't rise again tomorrow.

I walk into the house calling out her name. "Evie?"

"She's gone." A cold and recognisable voice makes my skin crawl. Her mother sits at the breakfast bar toying with a broken phone. She has a glass in front of her. It looks like water but smells like gin.

"Where is she?"

Recognition flames in her eyes, and her nostrils flare as she finally takes a good look at my face. "What did you do this time?"

"Me?"

"She was fine before she came down here."

"Evie wasn't fine. She was nowhere near fine, and, if

memory serves, you were the one who sent her here in the first place."

"You're right, I should have known better."

"What you should have known is how broken she is."

"That was mostly you and your vanishing act." She takes a sip, her eyes mocking, looking at me like I'm a stain on her pristine white walls. "I mean, don't get me wrong, I was grateful when you were finally out of the picture so she could have a shot at a real life, but you should have broken up with her like a man so she could stop pining over you for so long. God, it never ended."

I grind my teeth, my nails biting into my palms as my fists tighten. I don't bite. "I came back for her."

"You shouldn't have."

"You should have told her."

"I was looking after my daughter's interest."

"More like your own."

She stands up then and steps towards me, her finger pointing in my direction till it pokes my chest. "What could you have ever offered her?"

Her breath stinks of gin, and I step back reminding myself I'm not allowed to hit women. "Happiness."

"You can't eat that."

"We would have been fine."

Her laughter is as patronising as she is. "You would have been poor and hungry, and when she had a better income than you, you would have grown to resent each other. I saved you both."

"Those were our lives to live, our mistakes to make, our lessons to learn."

"No daughter of mine needed to learn those lessons."

I scoff. "And there it is..." I take a step towards her, crowding her space. I won't be intimidated by some broken old crone that wants to keep putting a wedge between Evie and me. "It's all about you. *My daughter.* Laughable. We both know it was never about her. It was only about how people saw you. You already had a disabled husband, God forbid you had a happy kid. No one could see her being happy with some idiot kid from a few towns away who could make her smile. She had to be dark and brooding just like you. Your misery needed company, and you knew just how to squeeze every drop of joy out of her life and take her down every chance you got."

"How dare you!"

"How dare I? How fucking dare you? You are her mother."

"And I always gave her what she wanted."

"Yeah? What about what she needed?" I'm huffing and towering over her, drowning in her gin breath.

She pushes away from me, and I allow her to walk away. A long angry silence grows between us like an abyss tearing open when the earth shakes.

She's back at the breakfast bar and no longer tries to hide her bottle as she pours another generous round and takes a long swig. "Why are you in my house?"

"I was going to fix it for you."

"You? You're the builder?"

"I presumed the name gave it away. Morrison Construction."

"Well, that explains everything." Her dry antagonising tone gets under my skin, and I'm willing my feet to remain cemented in place.

"What's that supposed to mean?"

"Exactly how it sounds; explains why your shoddy work-manship didn't stand against the storm."

I bite down my rebuke and clench my jaw, feeling every muscle tighten as if they are threads being pulled by a needle. I don't need to defend my workmanship and I won't. "You won't have to worry about that anymore."

She scoffs at me, and it's all I can do to keep from slamming my fists into one of her walls.

"Where is Evie?"

She shrugs. "She's gone. She seems to share your opinion of me."

I don't respond but storm out of the house and into my truck. My body is simmering with anger and indecision. I need to go after her, explain things. She needs to understand what she's asking. If I tell her the truth about Nessa... I shake my head and glare ahead at nothing in particular, my hands tightening over the steering wheel.

I can't leave Nessa alone either. It's been a week of back and forth, ditching my kid for Evie, putting myself first. I want so desperately to be selfish, but I can't. I slam the car back into drive and look at my list of other jobs I've set aside. It seems like my schedule has cleared up.

⁂

"F uck." I jerk my finger back and pain shoots through it before a deep throb sets in. I drop the hammer and grip it with my other hand, squeezing as if one pain would cancel the next.

I can't get my head into work, and this is the third stupid injury I have given myself this week. Evie hasn't returned any of my phone calls, and I can't seem to concentrate on anything.

Finishing early, I pick up my tools and make my way home. Nessa is sitting on the couch, her knees drawn up to her chin as she stares at her phone, her fingers flying over the screen. She glances up for a second. "You're home early."

"Have you finished your homework?" I growl at her.

"She drops her phone a little lower and gives me her attitude. "Yeah, I know your rules." She rolls her eyes at me.

"Stop giving me shit."

"Then you stop giving me shit." Her legs land on the floor and she's standing. "The whole week you've been grumpy and it's been my problem."

"I've just been busy, that storm damaged a lot of homes around here."

"Nah, it's something else. You've been tired-grumpy before, now you're just being a grumpy arsehole."

"Don't you dare talk to me like that!"

"Then stop whatever this is and be my dad again, cause I'm sick of living with you."

She spins around, and I watch her stomp upstairs, her door slamming violently in her wake. I sigh and drop my tool belt on the table with a thud. That's going to leave a mark.

Marching to the fridge, I grab a beer, twist the cap off and take a long sip. The sweltering air swims around me and the cold drink cools my burning insides. She's not wrong. I have been an arsehole and grumpy, and it has nothing to do with all this extra work that's been thrown my way and everything to do with Evie pulling off her disappearing act, avoiding all my phone calls and not responding to a single message I've sent.

This week has given me a tiny glance into what it must have been like for her. But fuck it, I hurt too. Telling her the truth will make things worse, but keeping it from her is a guarantee that I will never have her, and after the taste I've had, I can't let go—not again.

I rub my eyes, frustration dragging itself across my skin as I look up at the top of the stairs. I've never thought there'd be a time that I'd have to choose between my kid and the love of my life. I feel torn. This should be an easy choice; Nessa every time. But it's Evie, and every part of me demands I be selfish.

I finish my beer, setting the empty bottle down and watch a drop of condensation slide along the green glass like a tear. It picks up speed as it collects more water on its way down and pools at the bottom of the bottle leaving behind a translucent ring.

I draw in a breath and make my way upstairs. I stand outside her door and hate myself for what I'm about to do. I just hope she understands.

I lean against the door and rap on it gently, not surprised by her aggravated response. "Go away."

"We need to talk."

"I don't want to talk to you."

"I gathered." My fingers close around her doorknob. "I'm coming in."

Nessa is sitting on her bed, her legs curled up beneath her, her eyes glued to her fucking phone.

I step into her sanctuary and pretend not to see the pile of laundry gathered in one corner, her pencils and sketchbooks strewn across the floor with half-completed 'masterpieces', and her messy bed. I search her face. She looks so much like Addison; pretty and stubborn and so damn talented. I hope wherever she is she thinks I'm doing a good job, because most days, I just feel like I'm failing her.

"What?" She finally looks up and her attitude sobers me; it's the kind of tone that peels guilt away from you like paint thinners.

"I'm sorry."

"Huh?"

I grind my teeth cause I know my kid, she'll draw this out and make this exchange as annoying and unpleasant as she can, because she needs to feel like she's won, because she wants to punish me, and I probably deserve it, so I'll let her get away with it, this once. "I said I was sorry."

"Oh? What for?" She flutters her eyelids and keeps the rest of her face neutral.

"I have been an arsehole lately." I clench my fists by my sides and wonder how to navigate this conversation. "There are some things we need to talk about."

"Can it wait? I'm talking to Julie."

"No. It can't."

Her eyes narrow on me like I've once again incinerated her entire world, and she drops her phone with a dramatic *ugh*. "What is it then?"

I walk inside and sit on the side of the bed. Her mattress shifts under my weight, and she glares at me like I'm taking too long and she has better things to do. I look at her face, studying her deep brown eyes and pointy nose, the shock of brown hair and delicate cheekbones, and my heart squeezes in my chest. "I need to tell you about your parents."

The longer I talk, the angrier she becomes—not really the emotion I was expecting. Sadness, fear, maybe a little gratitude—but I'm greeted with a savage wrath perpetuated by her slew of teenage hormones.

"I can't believe you."

"Nessa—"

"No, you knew all this time and you've been lying to me my entire life."

"I had to, to protect you."

"To protect me or to hide me?"

"In this case they are one and the same."

"Whatever. You were just protecting yourself, and now that you've found someone you care about you're ready to ship me away, aren't you?"

"What are you talking about?"

"You think the whole town doesn't know about you and

that other woman? I've heard Julie's mum talk about it with her friends. You're disgusting."

"Nessa."

"No, you're a liar!"

I draw in a long, calming breath and let her anger sweep over me. She deserves these feelings and she will have them for a long time. My decisions robbed her of the truth, but I was a kid and I did the best I could for the both of us—one day she will see that too.

"Listen to me, you can't tell anyone about this—"

"You don't get to tell me what to do anymore—you're not my dad."

The words hit me like a frozen spear in the heart. "Nessa —this is important—"

"I don't care! I'm going to Julie's!"

"And when are you coming back?"

"Never!"

"Nessa—"

"Just leave me alone, *Liam*, I hate you!"

She runs out of the room, tears running down her young face and slicing my heart. I don't chase her; I know she will need some time to digest all this and face the reality of who she is and where she came from, and I hope that in that stew of hatred she will find forgiveness and realise I've only ever loved and cared for her.

The front door slams, and I fall onto her soft bed with a long, tired sigh before pushing the palms of my hands into my eyes. One down, one to go.

EVIE

I stare at the closet door. The white mirrors my emptiness, like leprosy that keeps chipping and eating away at my soul. I've kept myself busy all week, asking for all the work I can get, staying late to see just one more patient, watching them smile as they hear their baby's heartbeat on my monitor, or watching them tremble as I tell them I can't discuss what it is I see but that the doctor will call them in a few days. My heart bleeds for them as I know the disease has already spread too far and has done too much damage. It's like loneliness; it grips the most vulnerable parts of you and holds on, spreading inside you until it consumes anything that matters.

The nights I erase with alcohol till the darkness consumes me. My wretched heart longs for Liam; his smile, his touch, the way his smell overpowers and draws me in. I wish I could just leave him behind, but the anger follows me around like a monster in the shadows, and all I want is to scream and break everything.

Why propel him back into my life? Why throw me back into his arms just to get a diluted version of the truth and unspool the frail trust I managed to summon.

I fall back onto the bed, readying myself for another night of silence, when I hear the pounding at the door. It makes my heart lurch in my chest when a familiar voice accompanies the sound.

"Evie." Liam's voice booms in the silence and filters through the house. I want to tell him to go away, that I never want to see him again, but those are pathetic lies, so I stay silent instead.

"I'm not leaving till you open up." He keeps banging on the door, each vicious land of his fist on the wood reverberating through my heart.

"I know you're in there. Open up! We need to talk."

I don't want to open up. I don't want my heart to get tangled up in his lies, to be pulled by a thread that will have me sewing myself back into him. And yet, my legs won't listen, and my body won't cooperate as I slide off my bed and find myself making my way to the front door. The banging gets louder, but it could also be the harsh beating of my heart as my fingers curl around the doorknob. The sound of the banging stops.

I open the door just a crack to see him standing on the other side, his face twisted in a scowl as if he's somehow angry at me, like it's my fault he came to stand at my door. Like it's my fault he vanished. Like it's my fault he can't part with the truth.

"What are you doing here?" I find my voice and a shard of bravery that I hold up in self-defence.

"We need to talk."

"We've already tried that."

He ignores me and pushes on the door, forcing me backwards as he lets himself into my house. A house I shared with another man, where I made memories and tried to erase Liam.

"You should leave," I say, hanging on to the door, gripping it with whatever resistance I have left.

"I'm not going anywhere till we talk." He walks towards the lounge area and disappears, leaving me with silence. I draw in breath and close the door then follow him. He stands in the centre of the room looking at every detail of my life without him. The plush leather couch and large screen TV hanging on the wall, pictures of Trent and me spread along the floating shelves, the small coffee table with the single rim mark that stained the otherwise polished wood. He looks everywhere but at me.

"Would you like a drink?"

"No." His gaze drifts to me and floats over my face, his eyes lingering on my mouth a few seconds too long.

"Suit yourself." I walk away and to my kitchen where I get a glass, but before I can set it down, he's there and snatching it from me.

"I don't think you should drink either."

"You don't get any say in what I do."

His jaw clenches as he sets my glass down. "I have a lot to tell you."

"I can multitask." I grab the glass. Liam remains silent while I fill it with ice before free pouring gin and a splash of lemonade. I take a long sip, his eyes locked on my lips around the rim. "You have something to say?" The gin helps me keep my tone steady and uncaring; bravery in a glass. I'm pathetic.

"Can we sit?"

I nod and make my way back to the lounge aware of his presence as he follows close behind me. Too close.

I take a seat on the sofa and bring my legs up, setting my chin on my knees and hugging my legs. Another useless barrier.

The silence lingers between us, ugly and raw till my

stomach tightens and my legs shake. "Have you come to lie to me some more?" I finally blurt out, and I know I've hurt him in the way that he flinches and moves back a few inches like I've pushed him.

He shakes his head. "I never lied to you, Evie, there's just so much I couldn't say."

"Couldn't or wouldn't?" I bite back at him, the alcohol finally taking a grip of my tongue and lashing out.

"The truth is..." He runs his hand over his mouth like he wants to keep the words sealed inside. "The truth is dangerous."

"To who?"

"To me, to you, to Nessa."

There it is, that name again—that one point of contention that might never be right between us. "What about Addi? Is that why she never came back with you? Is that why she is still hiding?"

He squeezes his eyes shut, and when he opens them his face is a mask of pain and shame, and I'm almost overcome by a breathless longing to touch him, to comfort him, to go to him and promise that whatever it is—the source of his pain—I will extract it and make it all better. But I don't. I sit in silence and watch the pain slither down his body, hardening his shoulders and pulling them together, tugging on his neck as it drops, and his eyes follow his hands as they rub his thighs.

"The things I tell you, they can't leave this room." He doesn't look at me. His hands keep rubbing in a nervous pendulum till suddenly he stops and his eyes snap up to mine. "I need to hear you say that you understand me, Evie. It can never leave this room." His tone is cold and desperate all at once, and I nod.

"I promise."

He nods once. Then opens his mouth to talk, his face set in stone, his eyes drifting over memories.

"Liam, wake up, something is wrong." Addi's panicked voice draws me out of my sleep where Evie was in my arms and kissing my neck.

"Addi?"

She groans and grabs her stomach, doubling over. Her face is a wall of terror.

"Just hang on." I jump out of my bed and look for my shirt around our dingy little apartment. I've taken her away from everything, and despite all my efforts, I've managed to plunge her into a worse life than the one we had. At least back home she had her own room and some comfort. Here? She has a mattress on the floor and a fridge that buzzes loudly, keeping us up all night.

She makes another garbled, painful sound as I slip my shirt over my head. I splash some water over my face and run my hands through my hair trying to tame the strands before dashing out of the house.

I run to the phone at the corner and throw a few coins into the slot before calling for a cab, then rush back inside where my sister is writhing in pain, tears running down her cheeks.

"Liam, I'm scared," she says as I grab her ready packed bag and help her out the door where the cab is just pulling up. We scramble into the backseat, and the driver takes off, his headlights slicing through the darkness.

Addi moans in pain next to me, her breath coming out in short sharp pants that sear through me, and I feel so fucking helpless. All I can do is promise her that things will be okay and tell her to breathe. It sounds fucking pathetic as her face contorts and she keeps crying out. The cab driver tears through the streets and seems relieved when he gets us to the emergency room. I'm not sure he's concerned about my sister, rather his upholstery getting full of blood and bodily fluids.

I rush her inside, and the nurses usher us into a delivery room. There's a blur of activity as nurses and doctors rush into her room. I hold her hand and reassure her. She keeps crying in pain, and I keep looking into her eyes. Seeing my baby sister all torn up is killing me.

They tell her to push, and I see the exertion on her face, the deep etched tiredness as sweat slithers down her forehead.

She cries out and then there is silence as the nurses rush around the thing in their arms.

Addi lies there, her bewildered eyes searching the room. "Is she okay?"

The room rattles with the unfamiliar cry of a baby, and I look over to see the smiling nurses. "She's fine."

Addi visibly relaxes before her eyes close and machines start screaming. Her eyes droop shut and her breathing becomes shallow. Doctors rush to her side, and suddenly I'm being asked to leave the room as a frenzy of activity surrounds my sister.

They take me to a waiting room, but I don't want to be here. I want to be with Addi, I have to make sure she is safe. I fight the irresistible urge to call Evie; she would know how to make this better. She would know how to quell my racing heart and sooth the rising panic that strangles me. I have no idea what's going on, and I can't just sit. Just wait.

I scrub a hand over my face and feel the exhaustion as it drips inside me. I fall into a chair and stare at the pictures on the wall. Trees. I'm not sure if they're meant to symbolise anything, but they are old and faded and just like I feel. I find a black dot on one of the walls and stare. It sucks me in like a black hole daring me to look away. I do. I wonder what the hell is taking so long. What's happening? I keep waiting, jerking up each time a nurse or doctor rushes past the windows.

At some point, I start pacing again. I feel like a caged animal, but the cage is invisible and inside my head, and no matter how hard I try there is no escaping me. A deluge of thoughts and emotions floods my insides and my mind swings back and forth to *all the choices I made that have landed me here. I wish for a second I was still with Evie, that I was in her arms right now, kissing her. I wish that this baby was ours, the beginning of a family we once talked about. My stomach churns and twists at the painful thought as I keep pacing the room. I keep waiting.*

I'm back in the chair with my head in my hands. Eyes squeezed shut, a million different scenarios playing out in my head. I wait.

I don't hear the voice at first; it's muffled through the slew of thoughts that swirl inside me like a violent tornado.

"Mr Morrison?"

When I register my name, I look up to see a doctor standing before me. He looks grim, and my stomach drops. I jump out of the seat and face him. "How's Addi?"

"Would you like to sit, Mr Morrison?"

"No, I don't! How's Addi?"

"Mr Morrison, I'm Doctor Roberts, after the birth, Mrs Morrison experienced some complications."

I don't correct his mistake. "Complications?"

"Mrs Morrison experienced an amniotic fluid embolism—"

"A what?"

He explains the problem, but all I can hear are words like collapse and severe haemorrhaging.

I interrupt him again. "How is she? Is she okay?"

"Mr Morrison, I'm sorry, we did everything we could to help her, but the bleeding was too severe and we couldn't control—"

He's still talking, but I can no longer hear anything he's saying. Guilt chews at me like a hive of angry termites. Two lives that I've taken. My head swims.

My sister is dead.

"Is there anyone we can call?" the doctor asks.

I shake my head. There's no one.

He nods and looks at me uncertainly, chewing on his bottom lip and checking his clipboard for the hundredth time as if he has a speech written on the papers it holds. "Your baby is doing well. Would you like to see her?"

The baby?

It's like I've forgotten about its existence altogether. I don't respond. That kid isn't mine. Sure, I was going to be cool uncle Liam and help Addi get through the first few years, but now? What the fuck am I meant to do now?

"Someone will come in soon and take you to her." His hand rises like he wants to put it on my shoulder, then he wavers and it drops by his side. "I'm sorry for your loss," he says before turning and walking out of the room.

Everything is spinning out of control and a heavy curtain of helplessness drapes around me enveloping me in a dark shroud. The room spins and it feels as if the earth is dropping out from beneath my feet.

The door opens again and a nurse walks in. She beams at me, but I can see the caution in her eyes when she asks me if I'm ready to see my baby. It's not my fucking baby! I nod though and follow her out of the room. I feel automated, like I'm being driven by a remote control and have no real idea what I'm doing.

We come to a stop outside the nursery. Lined up bassinets with sleeping babies wrapped in blue and pink. The backdrop looks like a rainbow has vomited on it. I want to vomit too.

"There she is." She points at one of the babies, but all I notice is the tiny chip at the end of her fingernail and a fingerprint smeared on the window. She turns my attention to a door on the right. "If you go wait in there, I'll bring her to you." Her voice is so full of pity I want to claw out her voice box.

I nod and watch her unlock the door with her keycard before stepping inside and weaving her way through the line of sleeping babies. She reaches for Addi's little girl.

Addi's, not mine. That's not my fucking baby.

Anger and anguish seize me and wrap around me like barbed wire tearing at my skin. Without thinking, I turn around and *run. Finding the elevator, my fingers smash against the button, and I push inside as soon as the doors open, crashing into a man in a suit holding a bunch of flowers and grinning wildly. He gives me a quick glance, but when he sees my face he looks away and steps out. Fuck him.*

The elevator feels like a prison taking too long to allow for my escape. On the ground floor, I dash out and don't look back as I run out of the emergency doors and under the mid-morning sun. I suck in a few deep breaths and look around me. The parking lot is full of cars, and an ambulance stands unattended at the doors. The blue sky is too low, and the sun is too hot, and somewhere behind me is my sister's corpse and her fucking baby. I can't do this.

I make it all the way to the main road before I stop and look back.

"Fuck!" I scream at the universe. This isn't what was meant to happen.

He stops talking, his face drawn. He seems exhausted, like he'd poured out too much and is depleted. My heart jack-knives in my chest, and I reach for him. "Liam." His name sparks so much emotion in me; grief for our shared history, pain for our lost time, a deep ache for his mistakes and all the choices he felt he had to make, anger that he didn't ask for help, trepidation for what the truth might mean. But none of that matters now, not right now, not as I wrap my arms around him and hold him to me, not as his hands close around my waist in a vice grip and cling to me.

"Evie, I'm so sorry. I've made so many mistakes."

"I should have never stopped looking for you."

I feel his scoff against my chest as the sound tears

through me; it's cynical and sad. "You should have stopped earlier."

I push away from him and look into his eyes, they're glistening brightly in the light, a deep, hard sadness set around them. I shake my head. "No, I shouldn't have. Trent, he knew how to build a fire, but you, you know how to inflame my heart."

For a split second his eyes remain locked on mine as we stare at one another in a mounting silence that forces the air from the room. I look up at his face, the sharpness of his jaw, the hunger in his eyes, his lips. Before I can stop myself, I thread my hands behind his neck and run them up through his hair. His fingers dig into my hip a second before our mouths collide. He kisses like he's never kissed a girl before. Possessive and desperate and hungry, sending a shock of want and need through me. Our lips mash and teeth clink as our kiss grows more possessive, untamed. Neither of us have any control, our urgent desperation raging through us. Fingers clutching, heads tilting, entwined together by untamed desire.

When our lips separate, I feel the loss of his touch everywhere, stretching beneath my skin. But his lips only stay away long enough to rip my shirt from my body before he pushes me down onto the couch and presses himself into me. His hard cock grinds against me, and I kiss him on a moan, pressing myself into him.

His hand rips at my bra, pulling it off my body. Lowering his mouth, his teeth clamp then drag gently around a nipple. I moan, arching into him, and he does the same on the other side while my nails bite into his skin, tearing at his neck, shoulders and arms. He doesn't care. He explores with his lips and his teeth and his hands, and I allow him everything as the couch sticks to my back and his stubble scratches my belly and breasts and neck.

His thumbs tuck into the elastic of my underwear and he rips them away. His eyes no longer haunted, but demanding to see, to take, to have. And I want him to take—everything. There's an urgency to his movements like he can't have enough and it can't come quick enough, like he needs us to be moving faster before it all slips away again. His thumb sweeps my clit, and I moan, arching into him. He fumbles with his jeans and pulls them down, freeing his cock.

He kisses me again. His hard cock pulses at my entrance as he grinds himself into me. He breaks our kiss and looks into my eyes; he's either asking me or warning me, but either way I want him. He pushes into me, and I gasp at the feel of him. He grunts as he pulls me closer to him then pounds into me. It's not gentle or kind but brutal and unrelenting like a brewing storm, like the vicious sea, like I need him to be. I'm lost in sensation, my body rattled, aroused, on edge. It's a lethal combination that rips through me, allowing my orgasm to build as Liam pistons inside me, his strong hips slamming into me. I grind against him, lost in sensation. My entire body shudders as pleasure rips through me, and I try to draw him closer. I need him deeper still, but he doesn't allow me control, he continues to pound, to grind, to grunt until his rhythm becomes erratic and his body stills and his nails dig into my shoulders and his fists clench in my hair and his hot breath burns my skin, and with a final thrust he buries himself deep inside me, ripping a cry from my lips, forcing my nails into his skin, bowing my back, sending me reeling.

We're still and silent, only our breaths break the sudden hush that falls around us like snow. His face buried in my neck, he nuzzles the hot flesh as my body goes slack.

When he's regained his breath, he pulls away and pulls up his jeans. Without a word, he curls me into his arms, naked as I am, and draws me to his chest, then takes me away like a broken dirty princess back up to her high tower. He climbs the stairs to my bedroom, and I curl myself deeper into his embrace, drinking in his scent, his heat.

He sets me on the bed then climbs in. We lie there, in this place where time feels endless and unimportant. Where it's just him and me, where he gives me his shirt to cover up, so I can drown in his scent, where I trace my fingers on his chest drawing his tattoos like a dot to dot game.

I'm dressed in one of his oversized shirts. It falls over one of my shoulders and reaches midway to cover my thighs. We lie diagonally from one another, his head resting on his arm while the other draws long lines over my exposed legs. "I wish you would have told me sooner."

His eyes jerk up to mine and he sighs. "Me too, but you have to understand...."

"I do. And I don't."

He nods, he understands, and he doesn't.

"What was it like with you and Nessa? What made you come back?"

His hand freezes on my leg and snaps away as if I burned him. And for a second, he falls onto his back staring at the ceiling. "It wasn't easy. I had no idea what the hell I was doing, raising a kid... It was challenging...."

He sighs as if he's been holding the weight of the last fourteen years on his shoulders. He doesn't turn back when he starts talking again.

LIAM

*W*e spend the first seven years in hiding. Paranoia is a vicious bitch, and she follows you around wherever you go. As soon as people become too familiar, as soon as they start to ask too many questions, we vanish. Looking back that probably wasn't the smartest thing to do, but I can admit to myself that I wasn't very smart back then. All I had to go on were TV shows and basic needs to survive and keep my little niece safe. All we had was each other.

The problem was that once Nessa hit seven, she wasn't only talking, she was curious and asking a million questions a minute about the world around her. Why can't we stay? Why can't she sleepover at a friend's house? Why do we change houses and cities all the time? The only answers I have for her are about her mother and even they are a muddled version of the truth. The rest are complicated, and the more she asks the more her friends ask and the more the paranoia digs its claws into me.

She needs school and an education; she needs friends and a 'normal'. She needs a home not just a house to sleep in for a few months at a time.

I drop her off at school and make my way to the centre of town. It's small enough to be secure and big enough to not have a *small-town mentality. We've managed to stay here rather unseen for the last six months, but Nessa is getting needy and I'm getting restless. People are trying to get too close again, asking too many questions, wanting to know about our past and about Nessa's mum. I'm not sure how long I can keep feeding everyone the lie.*

The post office is also the only internet provider in town. I pay the woman at the counter for a full hour and go sit at the computer. It's old and slow and in desperate need of an upgrade, but for now, it's more than I need. I open up the search engine and type in Angel Falls, death, and the date; all of it seared into my memory like a brand. I blow out a breath and press enter.

The old machine takes forever to load, my stomach coils, and I can't help but throw glances over my shoulder at the woman who stands behind the counter and pretends not to be paying any attention to me.

The results come up and I scan the news articles from that day. Nothing about a man dying in a toilet cubicle. I search more dates, and more newspapers, spanning out to the nearest city, and still, I find nothing. I spent forty-five minutes poring over old newspapers and obituaries; there isn't a single mention of a suspicious death of the man that attacked Addi that day. Her father.

A shiver runs through me, a concoction of mixed feelings and anger that simmers like water over a hot pan under my skin. What if I've been running from nothing all these years? What if no one is looking for me? What if I am not a murderer after all? What if all these years I could have gone back to Evie? The thoughts lance me like a blunt knife and twist in my chest.

My fingers hover over the keyboard and before I can stop myself, I search for her name. Her profile comes up and my heart leaps. It's been four years since I've allowed myself to look. Her profile picture is nothing but some daffodils in the rain and the long background is a stormy beach. The picture stirs something inside me, and I push down the feeling. Stormy seas make memories tumble inside me like violent waves. The profile is set to private and there's nothing more for me to see. I'm somewhere between relieved and disappointed.

I scroll down through her old profile pictures just to be sure. The only other one that's there is the one of the two of us. The one where she looks at me like I am the centre of her universe. I gulp down the rising tide of emotion that has my fingers trembling and ask the woman at the counter if she can print a picture for me. She gives me a sideways look before nodding, and I download the image.

Before logging off I do one final search, inputting my father's name into the search bar. What I find flattens me. I clear all the cookies and search history before making my way down to the counter.

The woman studies the picture for what feels like too long. "Holiday pictures?" she asks before finally handing it over.

"Something like that." I pay and tuck the picture into my wallet.

Stepping out of the post office, everything feels a little different, like the air is lighter and the sun is brighter and maybe, just maybe, I can be free. A glimpse of a future I never thought I could have starts playing in my mind like an old movie.

Instead of going to work I go back to our shitty apartment and pack up our shit. There's not much, but now that we can go home, that will all change. I throw our things into the rusty decrepit car I managed to buy a few years back and make my way to Nessa's school. I know I'm being foolish, rash even, but the possibility of being free, having Evie in my arms again, floods me, floors me. I'm overwhelmed with a giddy happiness I haven't felt in years. I park outside her school and let my head fall back into the seat. The sun and the tranquillity soak right into my bones. Closing my eyes, I savour the moment. I want to remember this, to ink this feeling into my skin. For the first time in forever my body and my mind relax, and I can taste life again.

Nessa isn't happy about leaving school early, and when she sees the car all packed up, she folds her arms across her chest and refuses to get into the car.

"Get in the car, Nessa."

"No." She pouts, her second-hand school uniform hangs off her and she looks just like Addi. Sadness tugs at my heart and I round the car, going to her. "I don't want to leave."

I bend on one knee so that I can be eye level with her and tuck a loose strand of hair behind her ear. "Please, Ness."

"But I have friends here. I don't want to leave again."

"I know, baby, but we need to go."

"We always need to go." She stomps her little foot and her eyes well up with tears.

"This is the last time. We're going home."

"Home?"

"Yes, home." The possibility of a home blooms with a vicious hope inside me as I see her face light up.

Her jaw wobbles, and I see how hard she's trying to be brave. I gather her into me and hold her close, my heart splintering with love and sadness.

"Ready?" I ask when we break apart.

She takes a long, wistful look at the school where her whole life revolves and gives me a tiny nod.

I smile at her and open the passenger side door. She climbs in silently and fiddles with her belt before clicking it in. The school bell rings and kids pour out of the school building and into the yard where they spread out like ants huddling in small groups.

"Ready?" I ask again, my body itching to get going.

She bites her lower lip and stares at the other children, chattering and giggling and living totally normal lives. She draws in a long breath as a tear slides down her face, slicing my heart in two. "Yes," she whispers, and I selfishly take off.

EVIE

"I drove straight to your house, Evie. You were the only person I wanted to see, the rest...well, you know what happened..."

The silence is back to hug us, "It's been hard for you."

"And you too, Evie." His eyes latch onto mine. "I wish I could take it all back, but I can't; what's done is done and all we have now is the future."

"We?"

"Always, Evie, there's never been a time that it wasn't *we*."

Heat coats my cheeks at the words and fills me with a brutal wave of longing and desire. "Always," I whisper, watching as he shifts back onto his side and his hand is back trailing long lines over my legs making my skin bloom in goosebumps. His eyes track a slow line from my toes to where my pussy is covered with a bit of fabric of his t-shirt. He bites his lower lip and sucks it in as if he's thinking of something, and his eyes heat up making me squirm as moisture pools between my legs. He's trying to distract me. I shuffle away, but he grabs my arse and holds me in place, pulling me a little closer to his face. "I still have so many questions..."

"I know you do, but can you let it go? Just for tonight, and tomorrow..."

"What will change tomorrow?" I ask as his hot, soft lips kiss my thigh and try to make all my thoughts evaporate.

"I'll tell you in the morning." He begins to draw the shirt away with care, rolling it over my legs and arse as if it were a bandage. He kisses the other thigh and pulls my body even closer to his face where his nose nudges my pussy, and I swear he takes a slow sniff of my arousal. I want to pull away, but his hands hold my arse in place, and all I have is his hardening cock hidden in his boxers in my periphery. His soft lips drop a searing rain of kisses on my inner thighs as he breathes against my skin, a hot, burning wind that threatens to incinerate me as he brushes over my pussy again and again with soft whispered touches, reminding me of his presence. He's barely touching me, but I can still feel it all the way down to my bones. Making me feel crazy. Crazy good—intimate, a sensation I rarely felt with Trent.

My skin feverish with a deepening ache, my fingers mould around the hard shape of his cock, and I gently stroke his hard shaft. He growls against my pussy, a hot hungry breath fanning my growing need. I pull him out of his boxers and allow my hands to explore his cock, trace the bulging vein that pulses along the shaft, stroke the tight skin and watch as a bead of pre-cum leaks slowly from the tip. It's then that his tongue lashes out and makes my body hungry. I moan as my own tongue peeks out, and I lick the bead off the tip of his cock and slowly, meticulously lick around the head. His groan reverberates against my clit as he pushes his head deeper between my thighs, and his tongue draws long slow circles around my clit. I close my mouth around his tip and purr making him lose his rhythm and dig his fingers deeper into my arse. I can't help but smile around him as I slowly take the tip in and out of my mouth, letting my tongue play around the edges, licking, tasting, sucking, as his own tongue refuses to touch my clit, lashing around it in a maddening dance.

When I take him full into my mouth and suck him in as deep as I can, he lets out a deep, hungry growl and the muscles in his arse tighten and harden as if he is fighting with himself not to fuck my mouth. I wish I could see his eyes, but his head is buried deep between my legs. His tongue has finally relented and he lavishes my clit with slow lashes of his tongue, and I can't help but moan around him. Each time I do I send a shiver along his cock, and it erupts from him in a groan. We are an infinite circuit of sound and movement and desire.

I feel him growing and swelling in my mouth, and I work harder, sucking him deeper inside me, as his tongue laps and his lips kiss and his groans send me into a frenzy. His grasp tightens around me as I fight his grip to allow me to roll my hips and grind his mouth, but he won't let me. My nails dig into his arse as I gag around him, pulling him in deeper, losing my senses. My orgasm builds, rising, consuming me in pulses of electricity as his tongue is unrelenting, and I take him even deeper, wanting all of him inside me while my body shakes and trembles.

"Evie," he pants as his tongue leaves me, and I regress into nonsensical whimpers. "I'm going to come." He tries to pull away, but I refuse to let him, latching on harder and sucking him deeper, my fingers brushing his balls as they tighten in my grip.

His body jerks and a savage growl leaves his mouth as hot, salty cum coats my mouth and slides down my throat.

His hands clench my arse and hips push deeper into my mouth as I swallow.

Slowly, we disconnect. Our grips loosening, our breaths returning. As I lick my lips and fall onto my back, I realise we still have so many firsts.

"Pack your bags," I say to Evie as she sips her coffee.

She frowns over her cup and looks at me. "Why? Where are we going?"

"Home."

"I am home."

"You're not; your home is with me. This is a tomb of your past life, and it's time to say goodbye."

She puts her coffee down and stares at me, and suddenly I feel like everything I'm saying isn't obvious to her.

"I'm not leaving."

"You are." Her ignorance is her problem, and I'm about to fix that.

"I have a life here."

"You did, now your life is with Nessa and me."

"What about my job?"

"There's a new hospital in Angel Falls, you know they'd love to have you."

"I need to put in my notice."

I nod like I really care about what she is saying. I need to get back to work. I have jobs mounting up and clients starting to complain. But I know one thing; I'm not spending another second away from Evie.

"And my friends…"

"I have friends, take mine." She laughs a little at that. She wouldn't if she knew my only friend was Dylan and that all he'd ever want to do is get into her pants.

"The house…"

"Sell it." She is running out of excuses, and it's starting to make me giddy. There's just no way I'm going to let her off.

"What about Nessa?" At this I hesitate. Not because of the question but because of the sheer panic in Evie's face. I round the kitchen island where she stands, and I cage her in my arms, nuzzling her neck.

"What if she doesn't like me?"

"She will love you, Evie, how could you ever think she wouldn't?"

"Because I'm taking you away from her."

I graze the junction between her neck and shoulder with my teeth and make my way up to her ear, nibbling at her skin. She wiggles against me, trying to get away. "No one is taking me away from either of you."

I kick her legs slightly apart as I lean in closer to her, my cock coming to life as I get a whiff of her hair and taste her skin. She's fucking spectacular. No one can make my body come alive as eagerly and as quickly as Evie. My hands travel the length of her body that pushes instinctively into me, and I slide them along her side, my hand fisting the hem of her skirt as I keep kissing her neck and shoulders. My fingers drop to her leg and stroke the soft skin before reaching her underwear. I slip inside, groaning against her to find she's already wet, her body just as eager as mine. I spin her around, wanting her lips, easily capturing her mouth with mine, tasting her. Her hands jerk up to my hair, tugging. My fingers slide back into her underwear and in a second, I slide inside her ever so slowly. She whimpers against my mouth, urging me on, and I kiss her wildly, wanting to be even closer, to possess her.

Tearing her shirt open, I jerk up her bra and my mouth closes around her nipple, my teeth dragging against it. She tries to pull my head back, but it only urges me on. I bite down, and she shrieks, her nails clawing into my scalp. My fingers dip further inside her and my thumb finds her clit. I push in and out of her, dragging her nipple between my teeth just to clamp down again. Her furious pants urge me on, and I release her for a second so that I can pull down my pants. I roughly push her against the counter before pushing into her all the way to the hilt. A strangled gasp rips from her throat, and I cry out a ragged, pained sound that has my head spinning. She feels so fucking good. I hammer into her as her hands rake over me, trying to find purchase. But I just keep moving, fucking her hard, tasting her skin, biting, nipping, kissing her. Savage, vigorous thrusts that don't slow or relent, hammering and grinding with desperate urgency. My furious grunts pant at her ear. Her eyes roll back and she arches her back, her skin tinted in a dark shade of red. I'm totally enamoured by her; her raw, wild beauty, her soft breaths turning into desperate moans before her whole body clenches down around me.

"Fuck." Heat shoots through my body and collects in my belly before everything clenches, and for a second, I feel like a jackhammer has been taken to my body, but there is no pain, only pleasure as I come hard and fast into her, the sensation releasing like hot honey and skating across my skin.

Our noses slide together, my forehead on hers. Our ragged breath mingling as I grow soft inside her. "Now, go pack your bags."

EVIE

The man who leans against the canary-coloured Lamborghini is broad and tall and menacing. Even under the bright afternoon sun, he looks like a manifestation of a cartoon super villain gone wrong.

He watches us pull up into the driveway and remains leaning against the car. The knots in my stomach pull tighter. The trip up has been mostly silent. The silence seems to carry all the words between us; it's comfortable, mostly. My thoughts are with Nessa. I need her to accept me into their life, for her to understand, to be forgiving. There are too many emotions embroiled inside me, and no matter how many times I try to convince myself that it will be okay, a nagging feeling of trepidation sits with me the whole way up the coast.

"Stay in the car." Liam's voice cuts through my thoughts as my eyes lock with the man and his car. When did we stop?

Liam steps out and walks towards the man, who still remains leaning, as if we are the ones trespassing on his property.

The man pushes off and takes a single step towards Liam, who stands rock still—his body is stiff and rigid and his broad back is to me. I can see the muscles turn to stone as the two men exchange words. I don't know what they are saying, but it only takes a few minutes before the stranger climbs into his car and drives off. Liam doesn't move after the car takes off but stares off into the darkening skies, his hands wrapped around his nape.

Stepping out of the car, I make my way to him. He startles when I place a hand around his waist. "What was that about?"

He shakes his head, his face a dark thunderous cloud.

"Liam?" Apprehension filters through me. "Who was that? What did he want?"

His jaw clenches for a beat before he grinds out, "That was the guy I left on a toilet floor for dead once." With that, he walks away and into the house, slamming the door behind him.

I follow Liam into the house where I find him bolting up the stairs. I run after him. "Liam, what are you doing?"

"We need to leave."

"Leave? We just got here."

"And now we need to leave."

"Liam!" He spins around, his face slightly pale and his body strained.

He steps towards me. "I'm sorry. I shouldn't have come after you." Then he turns around and marches to his room, pulling out his phone.

"Liam, stop!" He doesn't. "What did he want?"

He doesn't answer me, instead, grabbing a bag from a

closet, he starts looking around the room and stuffing clothes into it.

"Liam!" I might as well be invisible; nothing seems to penetrate his shield. His ear is glued to the phone. No one picks up at the other end and he tries again.

I jump onto the bag on the bed and hold onto it. "Liam."

"Get off that." He's angry, but I know it's not at me.

"Talk to me."

"I shouldn't have come back for you, Evie. I shouldn't have gotten you involved."

"Stop talking like that. What did he want?"

He finally stops and looks at me as if he just remembered I was in the room and he sees me for the first time. He sighs a long drawn-out exhale. "He's looking for Addi."

A small gasp rips from my mouth, and I search his face where the lines around his eyes pull with strain. "Does he know about Nessa?"

"I don't know, only that Addi was pregnant when we left." he bites back at me. He plunges a hand into his hair and lets out a long breath before sitting on the bed next to me. His hand reaches out and cups my face. His is a mask of pain I want to erase with my kisses.

"What did he say?" I put my hand over his and lean into his touch.

He withdraws, leaving me cold. "He wants Addi and the baby she *owes* him."

"But Addi's gone."

"I told him that." His shoulders sag, and I can see the guilt gnawing at him, a hungry monster that he'll never stop feeding. "He doesn't believe me, said he'll be back every day till I produce her or his kid."

"How did he find you?"

He stays quiet, not meeting my eyes.

"The man from the pub the other night? They're what

you might call 'associates'. Seems he doesn't like his business partners being made fools of in front of a crowd. They asked around, most people in town know who I am; I wasn't hard to track down."

I let out a harsh breath and guilt floods me with its hunger. "Shit, Liam, I'm so sorry.'

He shakes his head. "It's not your fault."

"Of course it is."

"I've spent years looking over my shoulder, Evie, he would have found me eventually."

I give him a shaky nod. "You can take him to Addi's grave, prove to him—"

"No."

"But—"

"No! If he even catches a whiff of Nessa..." He shakes his head furiously. "We need to leave."

He's back on his feet and rummaging in his closet.

"Liam, stop." He looks at me again, but his body shivers like bolts of electricity are humming inside him. "There has to be another way."

"There is no other way, trust me."

"How can you be so sure? We can offer him money."

He laughs in my face and it's bitter and sad and angry, and it stabs me like an ice pick in the chest. "Pay him off? For what? To keep my daughter safe from her real father? He's a fucking criminal, a dangerous man."

"Liam—"

"You want to pay him off? What happens when he comes back again, and again, and again?" With each one of his words, he slices the distance between us, harsh and cold and like a blade until his face is right by mine. "How much is a life worth, Evie? How much should I offer him?"

I push him away from me. "Fuck you, Liam. I'm not your

enemy here, I'm just trying to help." I glide out of his way and out of the room making my way down the hall.

"You want to help?" His voice chases me from the room. "Pretend you don't know who we are when they come asking."

His words strike me like a lion with its fierce claws, simultaneously seizing and dismembering my heart. I run down the stairs. Maybe he's right; the only safe place is away from him. I should have never dropped my defences; I should have never trusted him again. The past leaves smudges on us all and contorts us into new people shaped by memories and pain, but Liam, he hasn't changed, he's still a coward, he'll always run.

A hand grips me and spins me around, and my back finds the wall with a brutal thud that has the air falling from me in a sharp, painful gasp. "Let me go!" I scream at him as I tug, trying to break away.

"No," he hisses in my face, and there's so much more than anger seething in that word. It's a heart-wrenching combination of anguish and guilt and fear.

He holds me there against the wall, and we both gulp lungfuls of air, waiting for calm to saturate us.

I push at his chest. "Coward," I snap at him, and he winces like I've lashed him with a whip.

"Evie," he starts, and I'm not sure I want to hear anything else he has to say. "You don't understand."

"No. You're right, I don't. You drag me here, you tell me you want to be together, you promise me 'always', and at the first sign of trouble you want to run off and leave me, again. I can't..."

My jaw wobbles as I think about life without Liam, about the emptiness that stands at the doorstep of my heart, a sledgehammer at the ready.

"I need to protect my daughter." He sounds defeated.

"I know." The anger filters out of me. "But what about us? Me?"

"Come with us."

"No. I won't spend my life running and hiding. I'm done running from my problems."

"Even if it's with me?"

"That's not fair," I whisper, and his hand falls away from mine.

"You're right, it's not fair. You can't make me choose between the two of you; she is my daughter and you're..." The words fall away as his eyes drop from my face. He takes a step back. "You're right, I shouldn't have asked you to come."

"Liam—"

"No, you're right, I shouldn't have asked. Your mum was probably right all along; you're better off without me." He turns back and reaches for the banister.

"No!" He spins around to look at me. "I refuse to live in a world where my mother is right, about anything, and you, you are it for me. How many more times can I tell you? Show you? What must I do to prove to you that you're my forever?"

He grabs the back of his neck, his knuckles whitening as he squeezes. "You don't have to prove anything, Evie, but if you won't come with me, we won't be seeing each other again."

It sounds like a threat disguised as fact, and it pulls at my frayed heartstrings. "You can't keep her safe by running." My voice sounds as broken as my insides.

"Of course I can."

I shake my head. "She's a teenager, she'll meet a guy, she'll want more, she has social media accounts. She won't let you keep her a prisoner."

"She won't be one."

"Of course she will. She'll live in a prison of your lies, and she'll fight you at every turn. She'll grow to resent you, she won't understand."

"I won't understand what?"

The voice has us both turning in the direction of the door where Nessa stands, narrow-eyed, her hands crossed over her chest.

"We need to leave," Liam says plainly, all the emotion drained from him.

"No."

"That's not a request."

"No, I'm not going anywhere."

"You don't have a choice."

"I do. I don't have to go anywhere with you. You can't make me, and you promised! You said we're going home, those were *your* words. You promised we could stay and be normal, that I can make friends and have roots."

"Nessa."

"You promised!" she screams at him in a high-pitched shriek that rattles the windows keeping out the darkening skies.

"Something's come up."

"Then fix it, like you always fix everything."

"I don't know if I can fix this." His eyes dart from her to me and back to Nessa who stands still defiant in the doorway.

"Have you tried?"

"Nessa." He brings a fist up to his face and purses his lips before dropping his hand. "You need to understand..."

"You promised," she says in finality before storming past the both of us and rushing upstairs, a door slamming in her wake a few seconds later.

He looks deflated, defeated. I want to go to him, but I don't. Anger still swims in my veins, refusing to leach out. In a few angry strides he burns the distance to his fridge and grabs a beer, unscrewing the lid and taking a long sip.

Putting the bottle down, he slumps over the kitchen island where he hangs his head for a few silent moments before turning to face me, his crazed brown hair over his brow. "Do you have any better ideas?"

LIAM

Nessa pushes the food around on her plate, her eyes keep glancing over at Evie, who shifts in her seat. Neither woman has touched much of their food, and the silence keeps tightening around us.

We did the introductions, and Nessa reluctantly agreed to sit with us for dinner. She's still angry at me, but she can't stay at Julie's forever and we both know that. She spends most of the evening ignoring both of us as we sit there exchanging looks. I don't know how to do this. I've never introduced any woman to Nessa; there's never been a need. There's never been anyone I would have considered to be around her, and even if I don't admit it, I'm a nervous fucking wreck. I need her to like Evie, to love her as much as I do, because as much as I love Evie, as much as I want her in my life for the rest of my life, I can't—won't do it if Nessa can't accept her.

"How was school today?" School is always a safe topic, easy.

"Fine," Nessa replies and stares down at her plate. I wish I had a stiffer drink.

"Just fine?"

"Yeah." She pushes the chicken around her plate and leaves it at that. The silence tightens around us.

"What's your favourite subject?" Evie asks, and Nessa looks up at her. I know that look—it's that 'what the fuck are you talking to me for' look. I've gotten it a lot the last few years.

"Why are you even here?"

"Nessa!" I growl, and Evie puts her hand on mine then flinches back as Nessa's glare lands on the contact.

"It's fine."

"It's not," I say and glare at my kid.

"Your dad and I used to be friends when we were kids."

"Friends?"

"Yeah, my granddad used to own a house down here and my parents would bring me down for the summer. Your dad was wild back then."

"Wild?" Nessa scoffs at the words and gives me a long disbelieving look. "*My* dad?"

"Sure." Evie laughs a little at the reaction, and I fold my arms across my chest. Great, now they are ganging up on me.

"How?" Nessa puts her fork down and leans back in her chair while Evie's mouth tips in a sexy shy smile. Her eyes dart over to me for a second. I'm not sure if she wants permission to continue with this ridiculous conversation or if she's just letting me know I'm about to look like a fool in front of my kid, either way I'm not liking where this conversation is going.

"He was a great surfer and a great dancer."

Nessa's eyes drift to me. "Dancer?"

"Sure, your dad used to have all the moves. He used to belt out all the wrong lyrics trying to impress all the girls."

Nessa laughs. "Wrong lyrics?"

"Mmhmm." Evie nods, and I scowl.

"I know all the lyrics to all the classics."

"Sure you do."

"Prove me wrong."

"It doesn't make a difference if we're naked or not?"

"Those are the lyrics!"

She giggles over my protest. "Make it or not!"

"According to you."

Evie bursts out laughing. "Sure, what about, excuse me while I kiss this guy?"

"I've never judged Jimi for his choice in lovers."

Evie shakes her head, her laughter contagious, spilling over to my daughter. "Calling Jamaica?"

"That's what he says!" I want to be irritated, but I can feel my frown pulling and my lips attempt to tip up. I fight the sensation, this ridicule is unacceptable.

"Here we are now, in containers?"

"Okay okay, you've made your point!" I fight my laughter, but it escapes. I may have had a few issues with lyrics back then.

"Are you sure, cause I can go on." Evie is laughing so hard her words are shaky.

"No, no, we get it." My frown is back, but it doesn't fool anyone around the table, and just like that, Evie has weaved some of her magic and the tension that strangled us moments ago slinks away like a child forced to go to their room.

"So how come you are back here now?" Nessa does a U-turn and like a dog with a bone, lassos the discomfort back into the room.

Evie's smile doesn't falter at the question though, and her eyes swing to mine. "My husband died, and my mum thought it would be a good idea for me to come here, to think."

"Your husband died?" Nessa's eyes grow a little wide, and some of the tension around her shoulders falls from her.

"He did."

"How did he die?"

I'm about to scream at my kid, give her a long speech about being sensitive and knowing better, when Evie leans in towards her. She beckons her with a finger and Nessa complies, moving in closer so they are both leaning over the table. Evie looks over her shoulder for added drama before whispering too loudly, "I killed him."

For a split-second Nessa's eyes grow wide and her mouth falls open just a fraction before she falls back into her chair, pouting. "No you didn't."

"How can you be sure?" Evie says, still leaning, then winks at her.

Nessa's eyes flick over to me, and I bite down hard, keeping my face schooled before I shrug.

"Ugh, whatever." She rolls her eyes and focuses back on Evie. "How long will you stay?"

It's Evie's turn to lean back into her chair, and some of the mischief falls away leaving behind a delicate, beautiful face. "I'm not sure yet. My grandad's house got damaged in the storm and your dad here promised to fix it for me."

At that, Nessa's shoulders pull back, and a small smile slithers across her face. "Yeah he's pretty good at that. He fixed this house for us."

My heart swells at her words, at how proud she seems when she speaks about me. It's tiny moments like this that make me feel like maybe I haven't failed her completely.

The rest of dinner is spent with sparse conversation; it's light and easy. Or at least Evie makes it seem easy when Nessa asks about her job and Evie explains the intricacies of looking at the human body through an ultrasound. I watch how the two of them interact. It's almost easy, it's almost natural. I feel hopeful.

Nessa leaves the table and retreats to her room with a last suspicious look, and I clear up the dishes.

"She's gorgeous," Evie says.

"Usually when she's asleep."

She elbows me and giggles, and I fucking love that sound. I love how she makes the house feel even more alive with her in it, like it's been waiting for her before it could really feel like a home. I hate that she has to go back to her mother's house.

"I better go."

I nod and I already miss her, even though she's still here. "I want to show you something," I say as I set the last plate into the drying rack and dry my hands on my jeans. "Come on."

"Where are we going?"

"Just come on."

She huffs and follows me out of the house and towards the back. "Where are we going?"

I don't answer; Evie in suspense is too sexy and way too much fun. I can see the wheels turning in her head, all the questions swirling around like tumbleweeds in a desert storm. She's anxious and curious and frustrated. Fuck she's stunning, and I'm fucking giddy showing her this. I've held onto it for so long wondering if I'd ever get this moment, and now that it's here my stomach knots and twists in crazy anticipation.

We get to the shed in the back; it's new and sturdy. I added it on after I finished the house when I realised it needed a work and storage space, and once I started working on Evie's house and realised her mum's plans for it, it filled up quickly.

We stand outside the shed, and Evie hops on her toes

bouncing like a little girl. The way it makes her tits bounce has me mesmerised for a second, forgetting why we're here. I shake my head, ripping my eyes away. "Close your eyes."

"Why?"

"Just—" I draw in a sharp breath, this girl makes it hard sometimes. "Close your eyes."

She pouts for a second then complies, standing perfectly still.

"Don't move now," I say as I pull out the keys and unlock the deadbolt sealing the shed doors.

"Hurry up."

"Patience!"

She huffs at me and her hands fist by her sides, opening and closing as she cocks her head towards the sound of the door sliding open.

"Keep them closed. I'm coming for you now." I walk towards her and reach for her hands. She jerks at the sudden touch. "Shhh, keep them closed now, Evie."

She complies, though I can see how hard she is struggling with this simple task. I walk her to the front of the shed and edge her over the threshold before I release her and take a small sideways step. I make her wait for a full minute, watching her face, the way her tongue juts out a little to lick her lips, and her jaw clenches making the muscles dance, the way she forces herself to keep her eyes shut by squeezing them tighter. It's a delicious delight watching her anticipation build, but as much as I'd like to keep her on edge, I know her patience won't last.

"Open your eyes, Evie."

She does and her eyelashes flutter as she opens and closes her eyes against the harsh light before scanning the room. As she does, recognition starts to form on her face, her eyes grow slightly larger, and her mouth falls open in a small gasp.

"Liam?" Her head whips to mine and I can't help but smile. "You kept everything?"

"I was hoping I'd be able to get it back to you someday." I'm not sure she's heard me as she takes another tentative step into the shed and glares at the large wooden canoe. It's the biggest thing in here and she would have recognised it from her grandfather's house instantly. The old man kept it upright against the wall in his lounge room. Not because he didn't have anywhere to keep it, but because he could use it on a whim. Evie would tell me how many times she'd played in it as a kid on a stormy day; how her grandad would take her fishing for imaginary rainbow trout. I think the old man kept it inside cos of the smell—it carried the ocean with it— it held on to the storms and the mists, to the brine and the salt. I think he hated living inside four walls; it's why he filled his house with the ocean.

She traces her fingers along the curved edge before her eyes glance over to the table in the far back and she makes her way to it, finding all the trinkets and pieces of memories I collected from her grandfather's house before ripping it to shreds.

"Liam..." She turns to me and her eyes are glistening. She keeps walking through the shed, her fingers brushing over dusty memories of a childhood with a man who meant the world to her. She's had so much happiness stolen from her. Watching a tear slide down her face fills my chest cavity with warmth. I know she's sad, but in that strange happy way people get to be when they are nostalgic about beautiful times. "I can't believe this. I thought all of it was lost."

"I knew how much it meant to you. Your mum never understood..."

She shakes her head before a sharp gasp is ripped from her mouth. "You kept this?" Her hands reach out, and her fingers brush over the old doorframe. It's faded and worn as it was when I ripped it out of her old bedroom, but the height lines are still there, solid and readable just as he marked them. Her height is forever preserved in his handwriting and skew lines drawn carelessly against the post.

There are no more words as she whips around and runs into me. I stumble back at the force as she throws her hands around me and her mouth finds mine. My hands fall around her like rope, and I draw her in, kissing her back frantically. Her hands snap to my hair and her nails claw my scalp, her body pushing itself against me as she steals my breath and sanity away. I want to strip her down and have her again. I want her everywhere, all the time. She makes me feel like the teenagers we used to be when lust was fed to us in spoonfuls by the hour, and all that mattered was the feel of skin on skin and lips on lips and getting that instant desire met by another person. She makes me feel insatiable.

When she pulls away, I don't want to let her go. I'm finding it harder and harder to let her go.

"This is amazing. I can't believe you kept it all."

"Are you happy?"

She nods, and I draw her into me, her hands wrapping around me and holding tight.

"Stay," I whisper to her, and she looks up at me, surprise colouring her features.

"Nessa..."

"—Will be okay."

She bites her lip in the way she does when she thinks things over. Then shakes her head and pulls herself away from me. "Not yet." I fall against the doorframe, disappointment washing over me like a bucket of cold water. I think back to those first days, when we were too young, and I had to hold off despite every part of me fighting not to jump her like a savage animal. She was worth the wait, but fuck, it'll be just as hard now as it was then.

She pushes up on her tiptoes and brushes her lips with mine before giving me a long look. I know all the words she doesn't say. I know she's right. But I still don't want her to go. Still, I watch her turn away and make her way to her car.

Damnit, I miss her already.

EVIE

I left Liam's place last night simultaneously happy and angry. I know he wants me, I know we can have a future together, but I also know I will never be his first choice. Not as long as Nessa is in danger, not as long as he feels responsible for us both, not as long as he'd rather push me away to keep me safe than be my safe harbour.

I roll onto my back, a light breeze sneaking in from under the tarp and pushing its way into my room. Summer will be over soon. I have an appointment at the hospital, a job interview. They were only too eager to hear that I was considering moving down here. They wanted to offer me the job on the spot before backtracking and saying something about a tour and the HR manager being pedantic about paperwork and procedures. I assured them it was fine, of course I wasn't going to accept over the phone anyway.

I get ready for the day and make my way to the hospital. The sun feels too bright and the sky too blue, like they're mocking me, showing me how everything could be when it's not.

I'm greeted by the head of radiology and the HR manager. They are both exuding over-friendliness and desperation. I wonder why they have had a hard time finding someone for this position. Blue Haven is a beautiful place to live, albeit overrun by tourists who spend drunken nights spewing in the ER and abusing the staff. Luckily, I won't have to deal with much of that, or at least that's one lie I can hold on to if I choose to accept.

We part on good terms, handshakes and promises—they will email me a contract and will give me as much time to think it over as I'd like—as long as it will be soon. If I read between the lines, they'd like an answer by the end of the week. I don't know where I'll be then; it feels like a lifetime away.

Driving back to Liam's I'm in a daze, my thoughts clouding the beautiful day. I'm so absorbed in my own thoughts I almost run over a band of teenagers crossing the road. They hurl abuse and give me the finger. I shrug it off almost regretting that I stopped.

My mind chugs a thousand miles a minute as I try to come up with ideas. How can we be together? All three of us? Safe, without always looking over our shoulders or paying out large sums of money to a criminal that would have no qualms about hurting us, or worse, trying to take Nessa away. My stomach folds in on itself thinking about all the terrible ways he could use her or hurt her.

I pull up to the house to find the Lamborghini parked in the driveway. The man isn't there and my heart sinks somewhere into the depths of my stomach and stops beating all together. I grip the steering wheel, looking around, and when I see nothing I climb out of the car. I clasp my hands together in front of me, trying to stop the sudden shaking that's taken control of my entire body.

I creep up to the house feeling invisible eyes on me. The sun is a beacon that highlights my hair and dress, and I feel vulnerable out in the open. I glue my back to the wall and creep along till I'm at the front door, straining my ears to listen for any noise. I hear none. My fingers wrap around the doorknob, and I open it, pushing it quietly before entering the house. It feels deserted.

"Liam?" I whisper in a husky voice and hate myself for being such a coward. When I get no response, I cross the room and make my way to the stairs. Hanging onto the railing as if it might save my life, I climb up, still cautious, still listening. I stop at the top of the stairs finding an empty hallway. Creeping along the walls, I find Nessa's room abandoned and Liam's empty. But before my heart dips into the abyss of my stomach and shatters, I glance out the window. Two figures stand outside. I recognise Liam's shape easily, the other is a hulking mass of human that towers over him as they exchange words near the cliff, away from prying eyes and ears.

I rush out of the house and towards the cliff side where the two men stand, the wind carrying their words away. Though I can't catch the words, the tone is full of wrath and disdain.

Liam's voice rises in the breeze. "She never belonged to you."

"That little bitch was mine and still is. She owes me."

"She owes you nothing, and I've already told you, she's gone." His voice still strains every time he mentions Addi's death.

"Well then *you* owe me."

"I owe you nothing."

"Leave him alone!" I find courage somewhere deep inside of me. Both men snap around to look at me, and I scold myself for not picking up some kind of weapon or having a better plan. What was I thinking?

"Well look at this. Who do we have here?"

"No one. She's not your concern." Liam gives me a look that questions my being there.

"Is that her?"

"Her?" Liam's face whirls back towards the man who leers at me.

"The cause of all this; the sexy dancer you stole from my associate."

"I stole nothing."

"That's not his version of events."

"He was drunk, his memory is flawed."

"She was basically dry humping him, which if you ask me makes her his, and now she is going to be mine." He pauses and scrubs a hand over his chin. "In fact, you seem to constantly be in the way of me and my women."

"Neither of them belonged to you."

"That ripe little cunt was all mine, and you had no right taking her from me."

"Don't you fucking dare talk about Addi like that."

"I bet this one's cunt is just as sweet. I think I'd like to have myself a little tas—"

Before he can finish his sentence, Liam launches at him, a fist connecting with the man's chin. He reacts, and in a second they are a flurry of moving fists and arms flying as each man tries to overcome the other.

My heart bashes against my breastbone and my stomach dips as I watch, horror creeping up inside me as the man's foot slides over the edge. Little pebbles tumble down the cliff as he grips onto Liam and rights himself, but with the movement he lands a devastating strike sending Liam to his knees. The man has the higher ground and keeps raining punches onto Liam.

There is no more room for thought. They have all been pushed out by sheer terror and grief and fear, and I run, my shoulder forward and my head down. My shoulder rattles and my bones shake as I connect with his solid body. For a split second it seems as if nothing happens, and then the world moves again in slow motion. The man's eyes snap open all the way, like someone is prying his eyelids apart. His neck muscles strain and cord as his head arches back in the path of a downward arc. His feet rise, leaving the ground like two kites. For a moment he seems powerless, grappling against gravity till his flailing hands reach out and he finds Liam, clutching onto him with all his might, gripping the collar of his shirt. It seems then that he is safe, that the fight will ensue, and my efforts were for nothing, till the slight rasp of material ripping tears through the air and Liam's shirt begins to fray. Pulling apart at the seams and ripping away from Liam's body, it leaves the man holding onto the fabric in his closed fist.

It's then that realisation dawns on him and his hands begin to flap by his sides, like a baby bird learning to fly. He lets out a strangled cry as his body plummets and vanishes beyond the rocks.

My heart thuds in my chest, a broken rhythm like a death toll of bells, and I rush to Liam's side, gripping onto him. His bloodied, swollen face is solemn as his eyes remain glued to the bottom of the cliffs. I follow the trajectory of his eyes where the man lies lifeless, one of his legs bent in a way legs aren't meant to bend. Chunks of his head are missing. His limbs splayed like roadkill.

I feel like I'm sinking. My chest squeezes tightly, and I can't breathe. I want to tear my eyes away and yet I can't quite look away. There's a loud, endless wail, and it takes me a few long moments to realise it's me. I'm screaming over the abyss as the waves begin to kiss away the blood of the dead man.

"Shhh, I've got you." His warm voice penetrates the cold that wraps itself around me. "It's okay, we're okay."

"Liam..." I clutch onto him, his bare torso against my wet cheeks, his collar and half his shirt hanging off him like a twisted clerical collar, but there is nothing holy about what I've just done.

"Evie. Evie, look at me." He cups my cheeks in his palms and forces my eyes up to his. How can he even look at me? "You need to get in your car and leave, now."

I shake my head. "No... I—"

"It's okay, let me deal with this. Just get in your car, and go home."

"No... I can't..."

"Evie, listen to me." His voice remains calm, though his eyes are thundering and strain mars his beautiful features. "I need to call the cops now, and I need you to be safe, away from here."

He begins to walk us away from the cliff and back toward the house where my car sits next to the Lamborghini.

"No, I killed him, I... he just...fell..."

"Shhh, just let me take care of this. You were never here."

"I can't lose you again. I thought he was—"

"I know, me too. You saved me. Now let me do the same for you. Go home, Evie. Now."

Liam guides us towards my car, holding me up on unsteady legs that want to buckle with each step. I keep trying to look back over my shoulder, waiting for the man to climb back up, to chase us, to hurt us, but he can't. His corpse is lying at the bottom of the cliff. The piece of beach that was always ours, always special, will never be the same again.

When we reach my car, Liam pries open the door and helps me slide into the driver's seat. "Evie." I stare at my hands, the hands of a killer and know that whatever I do now it will all be for the first time as a murderer. "Evie." His voice yanks me from my thoughts.

My head swings over to him. It feels heavy, lethargic, like it's not really connected to the rest of me. Like all my body parts are floating in pieces above me and act separately of their own accord. "Can you drive?" he asks, and I think I nod, but I'm not sure. I'm not sure if my face is cold because of the tears that streak down my cheeks or because the blood has drained completely away from it.

"Evie," he calls me again, and his voice is tainted with panic and uncertainty.

"I can't..." My shaky voice breaks through the fortress of my choked neck, and I suck in a long, shaky breath. I wonder if Liam felt this way that day that changed everything, the day he thought he killed this man, that I just pushed to his death.

"Evie. Evie, look at me." He's kneeling by the car, his knee in the dirt, his face stern, all fear and uncertainty wiped away. "You can and you will. Just like I did." I nod, my head still cupped in his palms. "Now wipe your tears away and pull yourself together. I need you to be strong now, stronger than you've ever been, and let me take care of this, just like you took care of me." I nod again, his words a soup of confusion that I try to digest and put together.

He pulls away and wipes the tears from my eyes as I suck in long gulps of air. He opens his mouth to say something when his head snaps to the side and he bolts up, swearing under his breath. "Stay here," he says as my heart flutters in my chest, and I grip the mirror to see a red Honda pulling up the driveway.

He plasters a smile on his face and walks towards it. The backdoor opens and Nessa steps out. He exchanges a few words with the driver and the woman behind the wheel smiles and nods, as if everything is still okay. As if there isn't a dead man lying at the bottom of the cliff.

I swipe at my wet face, drying off the tears and calming my breaths. There's nothing I can do for my stomach that feels like it's being squeezed by a fist, and I grip the steering wheel to stop my hands from shaking violently. Nessa walks towards the house, and Liam calls her asking her to come to his side. She's reluctant but does as he says. The Honda pulls away and disappears beyond the crest before Liam and Nessa make their way over to my car.

"Get in," he tells her, and she looks at him with a sour expression.

"Why?"

"Because I need you to go with Evie."

"Why?" She exudes teenage attitude, rolling her eyes.

"Just get in the car, Nessa, don't argue."

She scowls at him before giving me an annoyed look. When she sees my face her brows pull together and she turns to her dad. "Is she okay?"

"She's fine, now get in the car." His patience is wearing thin, as is my resolve.

Nessa slides into the passenger seat, and Liam leans over my still-open door. "Go straight home and stay there till you hear from me."

I nod, afraid to open my mouth in fear of what might escape.

He turns to Nessa. "Stay with Evie. Do what she says."

"Whatever." She huffs by my side and slams her back into the seat.

"Go, now." He shuts the door as I turn the ignition and slide the gear into drive.

I drive away, my clammy hands sliding off the steering wheel as my mind zips from one unrelated thought to another and my eyes flick from side to side, searching, maybe for a way to escape myself.

"Hey, are you okay?"

Her voice slices into my frenzied fog and sends my heart pounding.

"Yes, I'm fine." I don't sound as shaky as before.

"Are you sure? Cause you're kind of pale and sweaty. You're not going to pass out or anything, are you?" she persists.

I shake my head, not trusting myself to say anything, and Nessa keeps talking, or asking questions; it doesn't matter. My disjointed thoughts become disjointed words and sentences, and all I do is focus on my laboured breathing.

In.

Out.

In.

Out.

I'm still alive. He's not. Guilt and terror pinch my gut as a bead of sweat rolls down the side of my face.

I'm not entirely sure how we make it home, but I find myself in the kitchen. I need a vodka, a harsh spirit to cleanse my soul, but Nessa is here, and she already suspects something.

"Can I offer you something to drink?" I find Nessa nestled on my couch with her legs pulled up to her chest. Rabbit has jumped up beside her and is purring at her feet. She strokes him delicately. She tears her attention away from the cat and looks at me, really looks, her brown narrow eyes taking me in, like she's trying to see beyond the veil of flesh and bones then shakes her head.

"No thanks."

I go through the motions of making a coffee, my jittery hands spilling the ground powder everywhere as I stuff it into the machine. I take out a mug and it slips through my hands, shattering all over the floor, the ceramic pieces flying like shards of ice.

"Fuck," I swear under my breath before I start collecting the pieces.

"Here, let me help you." Nessa is there, her gaze holds mine for a few beats.

"Thanks, I guess I'm not feeling as well as I thought."

"Why did my dad send me here? With you?"

My hand freezes in mid-air like a bird tangled, in a snare, and I don't know how to lie to this girl, what the rules are. I swallow the rock in my throat, swallowing the truth along with it. "He has to take care of something."

"What?"

We're both kneeling on the floor, neither of us moving, our hands full of tiny piles of shattered porcelain and our eyes locked. I remain silent as her expression turns darker.

"Is he going to make us leave again?"

Shaking my head, I feel the tears pooling in my eyes. "I don't know." It's the first honest answer I can give her. *Let me take care of this, just like you took care of me.*

"Will you come with us?"

"Would you like me to?"

"I think my dad would." My heart floods with sudden warmth. "I think he likes you, more than the others."

The others. The warmth seeps away just as quickly as it was there.

"You're not like them," she continues on, "he looks at you differently."

I search her face for answers, not asking the obvious. "Your dad and I have a history."

"You were more than friends, weren't you?"

I nod. "He was the love of my life."

"Till I came along?"

"That's not what happened."

"Then what did?"

"You'll have to ask him."

I push myself up and throw the broken pieces into the bin. My body feels as if it has been filled with cement that's starting to set. Heavy feet, heavy bones; my head feels too heavy for my neck. I grip the counter for support.

"You don't look very well." Nessa is beside me disposing of her own broken pile.

"I think I ate something bad." I clutch my stomach as it starts to churn, my mind reeling with fresh raw memories. "Do you need anything?"

She shakes her head. "I have to do my homework."

I nod and feel the rush of heat as it tries to push itself up my throat. Rushing out of the room, I make it to my bedroom, slamming the door behind me before entering the ensuite and falling to my knees in front of the toilet. The vomit comes hard and fast, burning my mouth and throat in its wake. I draw in a ragged breath and wretch again, waves of nausea adding to my misery. My stomach lurches and gurgles as I empty my innards into the bowl.

When I am finally able to stand, I stagger to the sink to wash the sick from my mouth. But no matter how much water I gurgle and spit, the bitter taste remains; the unchangeable fact, the harsh ugly truth that nothing will change. I check my reflection in the mirror. Already my eyes seem haunted and the dark circles that were once a full-time feature beneath them have returned, making the long, drawn-in face almost unrecognisable. I wave my hand and the reflection waves back. I wish it didn't, then maybe I would be someone else.

A dozen needles dance their way across my forehead, and I search the cabinet above the sink for something to take the edge away. I can't drink, not with Nessa in the house, not when I don't know what's about to happen and if

I'll need my wits about me. I take a couple of headache pills wishing I had something stronger and splash my face for a final time before joining Nessa in the lounge.

She says nothing as I sit on the opposite side of the couch, but the slight widening of her eyes and the sudden flutter of her fingers over her slightly parted mouth tells me she sees it too. I am not okay.

I switch the TV on and settle in, waiting. I'm good at waiting. I've done it before, till it broke me. But this time I don't want to break, I don't want to wait. I don't want my fate in the hands of anyone else. I am the only one who gets to decide what happens. Just this one fucking time. I grind my jaw and square my shoulders as I keep glaring at the TV. This time is going to be different.

We eat a little, and it turns out I have less food than I thought and not enough to sustain an adult on a prolonged basis. Nessa says something about how she can see I've only recently been single, because I can't work out how to cook for one. I think she's trying to be nice, but all her words do is flood me with a sweeping arctic sadness.

We stay on the couch with blankets and silence and the TV humming. Nessa peeks at her phone almost as much as I do, but there is nothing, no word. So we wait. I wait till she falls asleep with Rabbit curled by her side and her breath is even and she feels safe, and that's when I leave.

***

The dark wraps itself around me like a blanket, but it has no warmth, no comfort. It feels like a leech sucking all the joy from me as the road winds ahead like a serpent. The stars have vanished under a sinew of clouds sewn together above me; another storm is brewing.

I know where I'm going, the direction I've chosen, and

yet the road feels longer, windier, somehow new and unfamiliar. I reach the driveway and slow down, the dirt crunching beneath the tyres. I cut the engine and look around. There is darkness in every direction. My eyes dart toward the cliff before snapping back to my hands locked on the steering wheel. Scanning the driveway, I notice the Lamborghini is gone. A cold shard of ice slithers down my insides and my head snaps towards the house. All the lights are off and there is no movement inside. A familiar feeling of déjà vu creeps around me like a dirty insect, and the more I try to shake it off the more I can feel it scratch against my skin.

My feet feel like they're welded to the floor as I stagger towards the house, my breath stumbling from my mouth in broken heaves that hurt my chest. "Liam?" I cry out into the night just to be answered by silence.

Gripping the door handle, I push down, surprised to find the house unlocked. The door swings open easily. "Liam?" I cry into the darkness and still there is nothing.

The emptiness that gripped me outside follows me around the house while I search the rooms and call for Liam knowing full well that he's gone.

There's a quickening in my chest as my entire body rumbles with an aching, haunted memory of pain. The pain and devastation he left behind the first time he vanished. I am consumed with a terrorising feeling, gripped in its clutches as it slithers inside me like a waking serpent that wants to sink its teeth into my very soul letting its poison consume every part of me.

My hands shake as I grip my phone and dial his number, and I go numb as it goes straight to voicemail.

I try again.

And again.

And again.

But all I get is the same message telling me the number is unavailable.

I slide against the door, sinking to the floor in a pathetic heap as the pain slashes at my insides. Cutting away the last frayed strings of trust and love, leaving behind a worn fabric of confusion and anger.

You saved me. Now let me do the same for you. His words sweep over me like an avalanche, freezing my insides. Is this his idea of salvation? Leaving me? And leaving Nessa? My heart dips as I think of the girl that sleeps on my couch. She's lost so much and now? How would I explain this to her?

The thought brings on a new wave of agony, like having a tooth extracted from the back of my mouth. The uprooting is suffocating, the pain excruciating, and all that's left is a cavity for your tongue to roll over and over again, pushing at the new scab, seeking the pain like a fresh reminder till your soul leaves your body.

Like a glutton for punishment, I reach for my phone one last time and dial his number. "Liam..." I whisper over the automated voice that answers.

LIAM

This all feels too familiar. The dark road in the middle of the night that slithers endlessly, full of possibilities. Life is all about choices. Oftentimes we take for granted that it's the big choices we make that determine our path; where we go to university, who we marry, children... But it's not just those choices that define us, it's every tiny choice in between; the mundane day-to-day decisions we make that really determine our everything. The right or the left path? Smile at that girl in the bar? Take the car or the train? Punch that fucking guy in the head till he falls and cracks his skull on the toilet base...

Every fucking thing we do leaves us with the next step we have to take and leads us to where we end up.

And I am here. Again. Driving in the darkness.

The sun glitters off the calm waves that lap at the sand. My head falls back, and I let the warmth kiss my face. When I look down and open my eyes, I find Nessa's face. She looks bored holding the fishing rod in her hand. The canoe rocks softly on the waves, and I think about how far we've come in the last year. She's comfortable with me, sees me as a confidant, as more than just Evie. There's a beautiful, serene pleasure in being accepted by a child. The trust they give you; it's fragile and beautiful and must be handled with care, because it's so precious and they choose to give it to you. It's been a tough year, for both of us, but resilience is built on the ruins of life, and we've built ourselves a beautiful fortress where we've found common ground and a place we can get along.

Her shriek takes me away from my reverie. "I've got one!" she cries out in a high-pitched voice, no doubt scaring away any other fish in the vicinity, and she starts to pull against her rod, shaking the canoe violently. I laugh a little and she throws me a scowl before turning back to her rod.

"Slow down, Nessa, let the fish tire himself out." I can practically feel her eyes roll even though I can't see them, but I also notice the tip of her tongue poking out the side and her brows pulling together the way they do when she's concentrating. "Just keep the rod at about forty-five degrees."

She does as instructed, and the canoe settles back down. The fish seems to have tired itself out, and Nessa seems ready to conquer this new adventure. "Get the rod up to ninety degrees now and reel in slowly."

She points the rod upwards and begins to reel the fish in slowly, while I grab the net, watching the creature try to escape. His shadow grows clearer as he comes nearer the boat, his shape more prominent, until before we know it, he is on the floor of the boat slapping and jumping about, and Nessa is shrieking with excitement and terror.

"I did it! I caught a fish!" I can't help but smile at her delight and get swept away by her enthusiasm. I remember the first time I caught my own fish and how my grandfather took me into his arms, how he smelt just like the ocean we were rocking on and how his pride penetrated my skin and warmed me up better than the sun.

"Should we go cook it?"

Nessa's nose scrunches for a second before she nods. I can't help but laugh at her antics. "Dad would have loved this." My heart flutters at the words, and I nod as I grab the oars. He would have, but he's not here.

LIAM

I watch my girls from my vantage point; they've come so far. Nessa has accepted Evie into her life just like I knew she would. They share laughter and a quiet moment. The boat bobs on the water, and Nessa's shriek is carried by the soft breeze as Evie starts to talk. Nessa has caught a fish, the boat rocks with her movement, and joy colours her face as her laughter drifts towards me. I wish I was there at that moment, but I can't be. I have other responsibilities. I turn away and let them have their moment.

The oars hit the water and we glide over the bobbing waves. We're not far off the shore and soon the bigger waves catch us and push us towards the beach. I jump out of the boat and manoeuvre us towards the sand where Nessa hops out, and we drag the boat on to the beach. Nessa gives me a questioning look and I smile and nod. "Go."

Grabbing the bucket from the canoe, she runs towards the figure standing near the BBQ, a thin trail of smoke rising from the hot coals cooking our lunch. She sprints towards him then halts before shoving the bucket in his face. He smiles then wraps his arms around her, pulling her to him. Our eyes collide across the burning sand, and heat slithers inside me like hot honey colouring my insides with joy.

I flip the canoe over and walk over to the both of them. Liam is glowing with pride as Nessa is still telling him about the fish. He laughs and pays attention, always attentive, always giving her what she needs. I know she appreciates it, because I know how much I do too. How his intense attentiveness makes me feel when it's just us, when he looks at me like he is ready to devour each part of me, like he clings on to every word I say as if it is the most important and riveting words there are, even if I am only talking about the shopping list.

He gathers me into his arms and sweeps a hand over my back before bending me backwards and kissing me, hard. His tongue sweeps beyond my lips, possessing me, as if he hasn't kissed me in years. As if he didn't spend a good portion of this morning lavishing my body with attention. My body heats at the thought as my hands grip his hair and dig into his scalp.

"Get a room. I thought we had an agreement about the PDA crap." Nessa, as always, says her piece, but Liam doesn't release me, not until he is done kissing me the way I deserve to be kissed.

"We're celebrating." He winks at his daughter who opens her mouth, puts a finger at its entrance and goes on to make retching sounds. Liam bursts into laughter and his arms squeeze around my shoulder. "You did good, kiddo."

"Whatever." She pretends to scowl, but the proud smile escapes, if only a little. She grabs her phone and hides her happiness behind the screen, leaving the two of us to tend to the rest of lunch.

As soon as she has her back to us, Liam kisses me again, his hand scooping my arse cheek and giving it a hard squeeze. I yelp into his mouth, and he laughs at me before releasing me and turning towards the charred things that were once meat on the BBQ.

"You might as well have come with us." I cock my head towards the remains of our food and am suddenly thankful for the fish Nessa caught.

"What are you saying?"

"I think you should just admit that you have no barbequing skills." I giggle.

"Are you trying to hurt my feelings?" He mocks a pout that makes me want to suck on his lips.

I take a step closer to him and slide my hand along his slick naked back. "You make up for it with all your other talents."

He whips his head towards me, and a heated look crosses his face. "Well if you keep saying nice things like that, I just might show you some of those later."

Before I can answer, Nessa interrupts again, hollering at us to give her eyes a break. We fall into laughter, and I release him, setting out the lunch and thinking back to that night where I thought my world ended again. When I thought he was gone for good.

Light washes briefly over me as gravel crunches in the distance. I am a limp mess of flesh and bones left discarded like roadkill to be pecked upon by the insects and scavengers. Soon there will be nothing left of me. There is more noise, like the slamming of a car door and footsteps, and then there is the impossible.

"Evie? Evie, what are you doing here?"

His voice sounds muffled inside my hazy brain. "Liam?" I lift my head from my arms and look at his face, his features twisted with concern.

"What happened? Where is Nessa?" He looks around, but his hand doesn't leave my shoulder, like he's a cord connected to the electricity and I'm in need of a recharge.

"Liam?" My hands move slowly like sheets in a breeze, and I cup his face, feeling the solidity of it, the whiskers of his beard, the warmness of his breath against my palm.

"Evie, what's happened, why are you here?" His voice is strained, and I feel the muscles on his jaw flex and jump beneath my palms.

"I waited..." My voice drops off and the rest of my fear settles between us, rough and cold like chipped stone.

"I had to take care of things..." he says as his grip tightens around my shoulder.

"You didn't pick up..."

"I was at the police station, they had questions... I just forgot to switch it back on."

I search his eyes as the crushing fear and betrayal seeps slowly away from my body, replaced by a tightening knot in my stomach that has my head swimming. I suck in a desperate breath to settle my churning body, but I can't seem to get enough air. My chest keeps squeezing tighter and tighter like I'm sucking air through a straw.

There is a feeling of weightlessness for a brief moment and then there is warmth; it wraps itself around me and smells like Liam, the ocean and sun, kissed by timber and earth. "Breathe, Evie, I've got you."

He rocks me against him, his heartbeat like a calming metronome vibrates through me, setting my own heart at ease. My lungs open and air floods my body as his words try to sooth me. The welded-up dam of tears erupts from me and slices my cheeks in violent rivulets. "I thought you were—"

"I know, but I'm not going anywhere."

"I pushed him, he just..."

"It was an accident, the police know it too. It's fine, we're fine, just breathe, Evie. I've got you."

The smoke stings my eyes as sharply as the memory, and they tear up as I watch Liam plate the charred remains of our lunch.

We sit and eat watching the parade of tourists that has slowly dwindled as the summer comes to an end. When we're done, we pack up the car and go back to my grandfather's house. *Our* house. The house that Liam is busy renovating to make it feel like a home. After my mother's dismissal of Liam, she quickly came to the realisation that all the other builders were booked due to damages suffered in the storm or were overpriced. She begged Liam to come back. That must have been hard for her, and the idea of it makes me smile. Liam agreed on the condition that we can design it and decorate it in the way that we want and that she allows the three of us to move in there. I never could go back to the cliff side.

At home, Nessa goes to her room, followed by that traitor Rabbit who has taken to sleeping on her bed. I'm glad they have each other. Liam and I unpack, clean up and make our way upstairs. The expansion doubled the size of the house and gives Nessa and us plenty of room. I love that Liam has brought back pieces of my childhood into the house, including that doorframe with the height marks, but we've also put our own stamp on it, building the house we always wanted.

I collapse on the bed, heat and exhaustion taking their toll.

Liam slips onto the bed behind me, his warm body sending heat along my skin. His breaths are harsh and sharp while my heart rattles in my chest. The weight of his hand latches onto my chin before his hand slips down my throat, fingers feathering my skin. His hand dips, skating along my collarbone. He takes his time like he's building a memory of me. He releases the knots of my bikini top, and it falls away from my body leaving me exposed. I shudder as his hand glides down around the side of my breast, and I moan at the ghosted touches. Wanting him hurts almost as much as having him.

He caresses my breast, his hand closing around it, his thumb gliding over a nipple. It hardens under his touch. He's strong and gentle all at once. Unyielding. I cry out when he pinches. It's unexpected and it hurts. The punishing sting spreads around and sends pleasure to my pussy.

He sucks in the sounds with a low grumble in his chest then continues his exploration. His hand slides down, fingers skate along my belly. I squirm, curling against him, and he chuckles. His hot breath fans my shoulder where his teeth sink in and graze the skin. His hand slides along my thigh, nails bite into me. I hiss and his teeth sink just a little deeper.

His fingers slither back up and creep to the elastic of my bikini bottoms. He pulls me closer to him, gluing my body to his. His chest hair tickles my back and his hand cords around me like chains before his hand pushes through the fabric boundaries. Fingers brush through the hair and dip into my wetness. I expect the touch and yet I whimper when his fingers slide into me. So easily. His fingers swirl and his hard cock digs into my arse as he presses against me making sure I know how hard he is.

"You feel so good," he rasps against my skin, making the thrill of my heart kick up.

His fingers sink deeper inside me, stealing more air from my lungs. He dips in and out of me in slow, languishing strokes. His fingers taunt, swipe, tease. I'm feverish with need, aching for release. My head falls against his hard chest, and I moan, and he lets loose a guttural sound that makes the hair on my body stand, like my pleasure is his. It builds inside me, heat and pleasure. There's a peak. I'm so close. I'm ready to tumble, but he pulls away tearing a disappointed whimper from me, but before I grow used to the emptiness his fingers left behind, he pushes his hard cock into me. He growls as he fills me and pushes deeper and harder, his fingers clawing at my skin as if he needs more of me.

He stills inside me for a few beats, drawing me close, moulding me to him till we're almost one body. My body desires him with such savagery, I'm bound to him with flesh, and I'll never be able to untangle my heart from his.

"I love you, Liam." My harsh whisper is the last of my

breath, and it slices the quiet between us as he slams into me.

My body trembles as his teeth sink into my skin. His fingers circle my clit and his cock ploughs into me. He consumes all my senses, weakening me, breaking me, making me his with every second. I drown in him and a hungry desire to fall over the precipice grips me. My body is overwhelmed with sensation. It's too much, too big, all-consuming and still he's unrelenting.

"I love you too," he rasps and follows with a violent slam, and all my nerves ignite.

I'm so close my body shivers. My hips grind against his, my body seeks relief, his torment too great to resist. His thrusts become erratic, his fingers stroke my clit, circling, pushing, desperate. My senses reel and my breath halts as my vision darkens. The edge has never felt so sharp and so steep. And then with a final brutal slam, my orgasm smashes me to pieces. I come and draw air, and my body is over-whelmed as my pussy grinds against him. He jerks inside me, burying himself deeper as I squeeze around him. My breaths are short and sharp and desperate, and everything feels like it should. I am just where I was always meant to be.

He holds me till the last shudders fall away and my erratic breathing settles and my body feels like it might belong to me again, like gravity has remembered to pull it back down.

"I love you too, Evie," he repeats in his husky voice before he draws me to him, nuzzling my neck and holding me close. I fall asleep in his arms, in our home, in the place we've always belonged.

The thing about missing Liam, was that it was never a piece of the puzzle that was missing.

It was pieces of the pieces. The fabric that wove our lives

together became moth-eaten and torn, muddied by his absence. Not everything is meant to be, but Liam and I were always inevitable.

This is a story about a boy, a boy who was always mine.

If you enjoyed Liam and Evie's story, please consider leaving a review on Amazon and Goodreads.

A WORD FROM JANE

I would like to start by thanking you the reader, so much for reading! If you enjoyed the story, please
leave a review and recommend the book to any friend you think would love this story. You will have
my eternal love and gratitude.
A massive thank you to Tracey Caldwell, your input and encouragement has been amazing as always
you inspire me in more ways than one.
To K even though you drink the evil drink of Mars you always give me direction. You know what it all
means to me. Thank you x.

ABOUT THE AUTHOR

Jane Wynters doesn't quite know how to answer the question of "where are you from?" She's moved from place to place like a snowflake on the wind always searching for a safe place to land. She loves meeting new people and exploring new places. She loves reading, writing and conjuring new worlds from her imagination. Coffee is at the top of her food pyramid and she is fluent in three languages, her favourite being sarcasm.

Want to know more about the author and keep in touch? Get snippets of upcoming books and have a bit of twisted fun?

Come join me in Wonderland...